## CAN THE SADDLE CLUB RESCUE THEIR PARENTS IN TIME?

The current below had torn a small tree out of the bank by its roots and sent it floating downstream. Behind it, rushing toward The Saddle Club, was a big black cowboy hat with silver buckles and a leather strap.

"It's my father's hat!" Carole gasped.

The hat suddenly snagged on the sapling, and white water bubbled and splashed around it.

"Oh, no," Stevie cried as she gazed at Colonel Hanson's hat bobbing in the water. "Our parents must be in terrible trouble!"

# THE SADDLE CLUB

# SADDLEBAGS

## BONNIE BRYANT

A BANTAM SKYLARK BOOK
NEW YORK • TORONTO • LONDON • SYDNEY • AUCKLAND

RL 5, 009–012

SADDLEBAGS

A Skylark Book / March 1995

Skylark Books is a registered trademark of Bantam Books,
a division of Bantam Doubleday Dell Publishing Group, Inc.
Registered in the U.S. Patent and Trademark Office and elsewhere.

"The Saddle Club" is a trademark of Bonnie Bryant Hiller.
The Saddle Club design / logo, which consists of a riding crop and a riding
hat, is a trademark of Bantam Books.

All rights reserved.
Copyright © 1995 by Bonnie Bryant Hiller.
Cover art copyright © 1995 by Garin Baker.
No part of this book may be reproduced or transmitted
in any form or by any means, electronic or mechanical,
including photocopying, recording, or by any information
storage and retrieval system, without permission in
writing from the publisher.
For information address: Bantam Books.

If you purchased this book without a cover you should be aware that this book is
stolen property. It was reported as "unsold and destroyed" to the publisher and
neither the author nor the publisher has received any payment for this "stripped
book."

ISBN 0-553-48260-2

Published simultaneously in the United States and Canada

Bantam Books are published by Bantam Books, a division of Bantam Doubleday
Dell Publishing Group, Inc. Its trademark, consisting of the words "Bantam
Books" and the portrayal of a rooster, is Registered in U.S. Patent and Trade-
mark Office and in other countries. Marca Registrada. Bantam Books, 1540
Broadway, New York, New York 10036.

PRINTED IN THE UNITED STATES OF AMERICA

OPM     0  9  8  7  6  5  4  3  2  1

*I would like to express my special thanks
to Tina deVaron for her help
in the writing of this book.*

STEVIE LAKE HURRIED up the path to Pine Hollow Stables for the Saturday meeting of her Pony Club, Horse Wise. She looked at her watch. It was 10:59. Whew. She couldn't be late for Pony Club *this* week. Her riding instructor, Max Regnery, who also owned Pine Hollow, had warned her when she was late to last week's meeting. He had as hard a time with lateness as Stevie had with being on time.

Colonel Hanson, the father of one of Stevie's two best friends, Carole, was on his way down the path. "Morning, Stevie."

"Hi!" said Stevie. She gave him a high five. "Aren't you going in the wrong direction?" she asked. Colonel Hanson volunteered at Horse Wise every Saturday, so he should have been heading inside, not down to the parking lot.

"I left my clipboard in the car," he answered.

"Mmm-mmm, mustn't get sloppy," Stevie teased, shaking a finger at him. "See you inside—I don't want to be late." Colonel Hanson was one of Stevie's favorite people, and she loved clowning around with him, but today she couldn't take the time.

As Stevie continued on her way, the colonel called after her. "Oh, Stevie—will your folks be picking you up today?"

Stevie stopped and turned around. "Actually, the whole family's picking me up. We're all going to the airport."

"The airport? Wait a minute. Why do you need to go to the airport?"

"We're seeing my brother, Chad, off on a trip to Paris. Can you believe it? His French class is going for two whole weeks!" Stevie made a face. "I mean, school is closed for one week for spring break anyway, but I seri-

2

ously doubt they'll get any *studying* done that other week."

The colonel's eyes twinkled. "Do I detect a little jealousy?"

Stevie shook her head. "Actually I'm glad I'm staying home—I'll have the whole week to spend with Belle."

The colonel smiled knowingly. He was fully aware that nothing in the world made Stevie happier than being around horses—her own horse, Belle, in particular.

"Sounds like you've got it all figured out," he said, waving. "I'll see your folks after class."

"Class! Oh, no!" Stevie glanced at her watch as she raced up the path—11:12! "I can't believe it. I'm late again!"

When she reached Max's office, she opened the door as quietly as she could. Members of Horse Wise were sitting inside on chairs and on the floor. Max was standing in the back. He ignored Stevie as she tiptoed into the room. Judy Barker, the vet who treated the horses at Pine Hollow, was talking to the club members. She stopped speaking for a moment as Stevie slipped in between her two best friends, Carole Hanson and Lisa Atwood. The room was silent. To Stevie, the moment felt like an hour.

Max cleared his throat. Stevie knew it was meant for her.

Judy smiled and went on. "So, to recap what I said before, a horse who has been eating hay all winter should be allowed how much fresh grazing time at first?"

"No more than a half an hour a day," Carole answered, poking Stevie with her elbow. That had been one of the questions Stevie had called her with the night before.

Stevie was trying to listen. She had tons of questions about this topic. But something else kept gnawing at her. Why did Carole's father want to talk to her parents? No one knew better than Stevie herself that she was always getting into some kind of mischief or other. But what could this be? When Carole nudged her, a thought popped into her head: That's why the colonel's mad at me—I called too late last night. But I *had* to ask Carole about whether I should change Belle's feed now that it's springtime.

"Right. And how do you increase a horse's grazing time, Carole?" Judy asked.

This was another question Stevie had had the night before.

"Well, after a few days," answered Carole, "the

amount of fresh pasture time can be increased, but only very slowly, by fifteen minutes per day. That's to help the horse avoid colic."

The Pony Club members all listened and nodded. There were plenty of kids in the room, but Stevie, Lisa, and Carole were the only ones who were members of The Saddle Club. They had formed The Saddle Club themselves, and it had only two requirements for membership. First, each member had to be absolutely horse crazy. Second, they always had to be willing to help each other out of any jam.

That was why Carole and Lisa had been listening carefully to Judy's talk—so they could answer any questions Stevie might have about feeding Belle.

Stevie's parents had just recently given her Belle, a beautiful mare who was part Arabian and part Saddlebred. Stevie loved having her own horse, though she was finding out that it was a lot of work and responsibility. Horse owners needed to know many things, such as the proper amount to feed their horses.

Judy talked about feeding for a while longer, then stood up. "Believe it or not, I have more spring and summer health tips for horses. But first, let's break for our own spring feed!"

"Yeah!" everyone shouted.

"I'll get colic if I don't eat something soon," Stevie said to her friends.

"Ahem! I get colic too," came a serious, deep voice. It was Max. "From lateness, especially when it's one of my best riders."

Stevie blushed. "Sorry, Max," she said.

"This meeting started at eleven sharp, not eleven-fifteen," said Max, still annoyed. "Try being *early* next week, then maybe you'll be on time. And don't get *lost* during lunch break."

Stevie knew he was half joking. "Okay," she promised sheepishly. "I will. I mean, I won't. I'm sorry," she stammered.

She and her friends headed out of the office and over to their cubbies. Stevie could feel that her face was still red. She hated it when Max was annoyed at her.

"You know why I was late?" she said to her friends.

"Why?" asked Lisa and Carole as they headed outside to sit on a bale of hay and eat under the April sunshine.

"Because I was being interrogated by the marines!" Stevie sat down on the hay bale and took her sandwich out of the bag. "I bumped into your dad, Carole, and he wanted to know if my parents were picking me up today." She cast a worried look at her friend. "Was your father mad at me for calling last night?"

"Well, you did wake us both up," Carole admitted after swallowing a bite of her ham and cheese sandwich.

Lisa's eyes were wide. "I must be in trouble too," she said, sounding worried. "When I saw your father, he told me he wanted to talk to *my* parents." Lisa didn't get into trouble the way Stevie did. In fact, she was a straight-A student. She couldn't imagine what it was she might have done.

Stevie frowned. "Maybe it's from the time we turned your bathroom sink blue. Remember that diffusion experiment we did?"

Carole shook her head. "You can hardly notice it now. Besides, he already scolded me about that."

"Do you think he's going to tell them about all the bubble gum I chew?" Stevie went on. "I always do it at your house because Mom and Dad won't let me at home because of my braces. I keep breaking brackets. And if my parents knew—"

"How could it be about your braces," answered Lisa, "if he wants to see my parents too?"

That stopped Stevie short. The girls munched their

sandwiches in silence for a moment, mulling over the possibilities.

"Come to think of it," said Stevie, "your dad called and spoke to my mom a couple of weeks ago, and she never told me what it was about."

"That's weird," Lisa said. "I overheard my parents talking the other night, and I thought I heard my dad mention your dad's name. But I wasn't sure, and I definitely wasn't supposed to be listening, so I just dropped it." Lisa turned a little pale. "I hope it's nothing major. I hate when my mom gets upset. You know how overprotective she is."

A few minutes later Max's voice came booming over the P.A. system. "Your attention please. Horse Wise will resume in three minutes."

Stevie nearly choked on her drink. For now she was finished worrying about whatever Colonel Hanson wanted to tell her parents. She had something more immediate to worry about. She leapt up, balled up her sandwich bag, and tossed it in the trash. "I'd better not give Max colic," she yelled over her shoulder as she dashed into the barn. "I'm already in enough trouble."

Her two friends chuckled and followed her inside.

8

WHEN THE MEMBERS of The Saddle Club left the Horse Wise meeting later that afternoon, Colonel Hanson was deep in conversation with the other parents.

Stevie stopped dead in her tracks. "See what I mean? Something's definitely up!"

The grown-ups were standing beside the Lakes' station wagon. Stevie's brothers, Chad, her twin, Alex, and Michael were sitting inside, waiting.

As the girls approached, Stevie heard snatches of the conversation.

"Sugar airplane . . . ," she heard Colonel Hanson say.

"Greek spleedum . . . ," she thought was her father's answer. And then someone said something about a ban or a bun. Were they having an impromptu French lesson? She didn't get it. But at least no one looked angry.

"Hi, girls!" Colonel Hanson turned to them as they walked up.

"Is it my imagination," said Stevie, "or is there something fishy going on here?"

Her mother chuckled. "Well, it's not exactly fishy. Horsey's more like it. I think we ought to let Mitch break the good news."

"Well, I have a big surprise for all of you girls," the colonel began. "I even kept it a secret from my black-eyed beauty, Carole, here. This year's spring vacation plans include a trip on a private plane. To a certain part of Colorado—"

"The Bar None!" cried all three girls.

The Bar None was a dude ranch in Colorado, and the home of the girls' good friend Kate Devine. It was also The Saddle Club's favorite home away from home. The girls had made several visits out there already—in fact, they had formed a Western branch of The Saddle Club with Kate, whose parents, Phyllis and Frank, owned the ranch, and with Christine Lonetree, another horse-crazy girl who was a neighbor of Kate's.

Lisa, Carole, and Stevie let out whoops of delight and hugged and jumped up and down.

"I thought I was in trouble!" Stevie almost shouted, throwing her head back with a laugh.

"Why ever would *you* think that?" Mrs. Lake asked in mock surprise.

Lisa looked at Colonel Hanson, and then at her mother, and then back at Colonel Hanson, and caught her breath. "So all three of us are going?"

The parents got very quiet.

Colonel Hanson cleared his throat. "As a matter of fact, all eight of us are going."

The three girls looked at each other. Their parents were going to the Bar None? They broke out in grins all over again. Showing their parents the dude ranch would be so much fun.

*Hoonnnk!*

Alex was reaching over into the front seat of the Lakes' car, leaning on the horn. "C'mon, guys! Let's get going!" he called.

"Okay, just a minute!" said Mr. Lake.

"How long has this secret been kept from us?" Stevie asked.

Colonel Hanson began. "I'd been planning to surprise Carole with a trip out west for the two of us. Then, about two weeks ago, Frank called and said that a party of eight who'd reserved the same week had canceled. Apparently Kate had convinced him to suggest that the rest of The Saddle Club and their parents come along. So I made a couple of calls to your parents."

"And the only thing left to figure out," Mrs. Atwood told Lisa, "was whether your father and Stevie's parents could get time off from work."

"Until yesterday neither Stevie's mom nor I knew if we could get the time free," Mr. Atwood added. "But as of last night, we're all set."

"Wow!" said Lisa to her father. He was always so serious. But this time she could tell he was excited. "I can't believe it!"

"So that's what the phone call from Carole's dad was about," Stevie said to her mother, who smiled in response.

"So I guess *we'll* be the teachers!" Carole gave her father a poke in the ribs.

Colonel Hanson put his hands on his hips. "And just what do you mean by that?" he asked.

"She means," Stevie interjected, "that we'll get a chance to be the experts, and show you grown-ups what to do."

Colonel Hanson laughed. "Don't you do that enough already?" he asked.

"Not on horseback," answered Carole. "When do we leave?"

"One week from tomorrow," replied her father.

"This is so great," Lisa declared. "I can't wait to show you my favorite thing about the Bar None, Mom. We go on this bareback ride just before dawn and we watch the sun rise!"

Mrs. Atwood pursed her lips. "Sounds like a nice ride," she said. "But personally, I think I'd rather use a saddle."

"I think I'll stick to my favorite predawn activity— especially on vacation—sleeping," Mr. Atwood chimed in.

"It does sound a bit early," Mrs. Atwood agreed. "Do you think we could leave after breakfast instead?"

"For a sunrise ride, Mom?" Lisa shook her head.

*Beeep! Beep, Beeeeeep!*

"That's enough, boys," Mr. Lake yelled to Stevie's brothers. He shook the colonel's hand. "Well, Mitch, thanks for doing all this legwork. Right now, we'd better go, or Chad'll miss his plane and have to go to the Bar None instead of Paris!"

"No! No!" Stevie groaned. "A fate worse than death!"

Carole and Lisa laughed. They waved good-bye to Stevie.

As Lisa climbed into the backseat of her parents' car, she thought about their response to the sunrise bareback ride. Every time she stayed at the Bar None, the ride up into the mountains to see the sun rise over the majestic Rockies had thrilled her. Why weren't her parents more excited about the ride? Lisa sighed, hoping this wasn't an omen. At first Lisa had been happy that her parents had planned this wonderful trip. But by the time they pulled into their driveway, Lisa realized she had lots of mixed feelings. Her mother was so concerned about appearances and staying neat, she'd probably prefer a swimming pool and sauna to a dusty trail ride under the blazing western sun. Plus she couldn't imagine either of her parents interacting with Kate, Christine, *and* John

14

Brightstar, the young Native American Indian wrangler with whom she had a special friendship.

As Lisa climbed out of the car and headed into the house, an uneasy feeling settled in her stomach. Until they arrived in Colorado, she couldn't be sure how her parents were going to react to any of it—the horses, the rustic atmosphere, *and* her friendship with John.

"GOOD NIGHT, DAD," said Carole, giving her father a hug and kiss.

"Good night, hon."

"And thanks for the surprise. I can't wait to go!" Carole padded off to bed.

As she climbed in and pulled up the covers, the phone rang. She looked at her clock and shook her head: 11:02. It had to be Stevie.

Carole's father called down the hall. "For you, sweetheart. And tell Stevie, we're still on Eastern Standard Time!"

She knew it. Stevie. Carole went down to the kitchen and picked up.

"Well, we made it to the airport by the skin of our teeth," Stevie reported.

"I guess that means Chad won't be coming to the Bar None."

"Nope," Stevie answered. "And Alex and Michael will be at Boy Scout Camp. What a relief." She hesitated. "Sorry to call so late, but I just had to talk to you and Lisa."

"What's up?" asked Carole. She could hear the note of tension in Stevie's voice.

"To tell you the truth," Stevie went on, "I've been thinking about what it'll feel like to have our parents come to the Bar None. I mean, it's always been The Saddle Club. The three of us, and Kate and Christine. I guess I don't really want my parents *in* on everything."

Carole tried to reassure her. "Just because your parents are coming with us doesn't mean they have to know everything about what we do. They'll probably leave us alone sometimes and go off by themselves."

Stevie yawned. "Yeah. You're probably right. I still think it'll be fun to bring them along, but it might feel a little strange, that's all. I just hung up with Lisa. She's nervous about her mom and dad too."

"You two need to stop worrying so much," Carole said. "By the time we're packed and ready to go, I'm sure you'll be too excited to care who comes with us—even if it's your brothers."

Stevie laughed in spite of her worries. "Don't even suggest that!"

CAROLE THOUGHT THE following weekend would never arrive. All week long the trip to the Bar None was all she could think about. She couldn't wait to see Kate and Christine, plus she was excited about showing the Bar None to her father—even if he might embarrass her a little. Finally the day arrived.

On Sunday morning, as they were taking their suitcases out to the Lakes' car, Carole told her father about the strange dream she'd had the night before.

"You were riding this Appaloosa bareback," she said, "and you were galloping along, roping a runaway steer!"

"Sounds plausible," the colonel answered, his brown eyes twinkling.

"Get serious, Dad," Carole answered, "that's something even *I* couldn't do!"

She called hello to the Lakes and lifted her suitcase into the back of the station wagon. Her father had laughed about her dream, but Carole couldn't help wondering if he'd actually try some daredevil riding stunts like steer roping. She hoped not. Sometimes he liked to joke around and show off, but he didn't have nearly enough riding experience to tackle anything much beyond a trail ride.

When her friends pulled up in the Lakes' station wagon, Lisa was waiting impatiently on her front steps. She grabbed her duffel bag and ran down to stow it in the car.

"Mom's running a little late," she called, rolling her eyes. "She and Dad are having trouble closing the suitcase. I think she packed fourteen different outfits." She climbed into the back next to her friends. "Last night I had a dream about Mom making a disgusted face at Dad while Phyllis showed them their bunkhouse. Then she called the curtains quaint right to Phyllis's face!"

"You think that's bad," Carole said grimly. "I dreamt my father was acting like a rodeo daredevil!"

The girls exchanged uneasy glances.

"Maybe we can ignore them," Stevie began. "Maybe once we're out West they won't even—"

" 'Oh, give me a home, where the buffalo roam, and the deer—' "

Her father's cheerful voice crooning "Home on the

Range" interrupted Stevie's short-lived burst of optimism.

"Aaaaaaaagh!" cried Stevie.

Mr. Lake stopped singing. "What's wrong, honey? Don't you like my voice?"

"You just reminded me of a dream I had last night!" Stevie cried. "Actually, it was more like a nightmare!"

"Were we in it?" Stevie's mother asked. "Singing cowboy songs?"

"You were both singing 'The Streets of Laredo,' as a matter of fact!" was Stevie's reply. Everyone burst out laughing.

"Well, pardners, westward ho!" Mr. Lake called out. Then, while the three girls huddled in the back, hands over their ears, the rest of the parents joined in the song.

LISA SAT IN her favorite rocking chair on the porch of the girls' bunkhouse at the Bar None and looked out at the sky. It always surprised her how huge it was. She knew it was the same sky she saw in Willow Creek, but here it seemed to go on forever.

She sighed. Eight days ago she had no idea she'd be out here. Now here she was, with her best friends—*and her parents!* For a moment she stopped worrying about her mother or anticipating seeing John Brightstar. She simply enjoyed being back in this wonderful place. Lisa rocked in the chair and smiled.

A few minutes later Stevie and Carole joined her on the porch.

"I can't believe we're here!" exclaimed Stevie.

"Me neither," answered Carole, "and I can't wait to go for a ride!"

At that moment Kate rounded the corner to the bunkhouse. "How about right now?"

"Kate!" All three girls bounded off the porch to hug their friend. She looked the same as last time they'd seen her except maybe taller, her deep auburn hair pulled back in a ponytail.

"Sorry I couldn't meet you at the airport. I had this dumb dentist appointment—"

"That's okay," said Lisa.

"How are you?" Carole asked.

"Great, just a little numb," answered Kate, rubbing her jaw.

"Nothing a ride won't cure, right?" said Stevie.

"You got it." Kate grinned. "I'm so glad to see you guys."

"Hey, thanks for working on your dad to invite all of us," said Stevie.

"No problem," answered Kate. "I just had to agree to help train a couple of our new fillies."

The girls smiled. Kate was probably the most experienced rider of all of them, and they knew she'd love training the young horses.

"Let's go for that ride," said Stevie.

"Sounds good," said Lisa, "but let's check on our parents first. Maybe they'll want to come."

As they headed over to the parents' bunkhouse, Stevie turned to Kate. "So just how long did *you* know about this surprise?"

"Longer than any of you!" Kate replied.

"Do we ever owe you one," said Stevie. "Just you wait."

Kate laughed. "Uh-oh, I'd better watch out. I've heard lots of stories about Stevie Lake's revenge schemes—none of them pretty!"

"Hi!" called Mrs. Atwood as The Saddle Club walked up. To Lisa's surprise, her mother's face was glowing. "The view is great from every window, and I love this little porch."

"How'd you like to see the view from horseback?" Lisa asked.

Mrs. Atwood nodded. "Sounds good."

Stevie's mother appeared from inside the cabin. "Can I come too?"

"Of course!" Stevie answered, "Everyone's invited!"

"Let's all meet at the corral in twenty minutes, okay?" said Kate.

"See you there," Mrs. Atwood replied.

"I'll tell the dads in here," said Mrs. Lake.

"Speaking of dads, I want to go check on mine," said Carole. "He's up at the big house." The girls walked over to the main house, a long, low ranch with a porch that stretched across the front.

As they walked in, Phyllis Devine, Kate's mother, came out of the kitchen.

"Stevie! Carole! Lisa!" she said, hugging them each. "How're my favorite dudes? I'm so glad you brought your folks. Carole, your dad is staying in the guest room right down the hall from us."

Carole headed down the hall and met her father coming out of his room. He had changed into jeans and a Western shirt.

"Are you ready for a ride?" she asked.

"Does a coyote howl?" Colonel Hanson answered with a big smile.

"Meet us at the corral in fifteen minutes," Carole told him. Then she and her friends headed back outside.

As the others chattered away, Lisa kept her eyes

peeled for John Brightstar. He and his father, Walter, worked at the Bar None, and during her last couple of visits to the ranch she had become good friends with John.

She drew in a deep breath when she finally spotted the tall, black-haired wrangler coming out of the barn with his father.

Walter nodded. "Hello, girls," he said quietly.

John gave each of the three visitors a friendly hug—though it felt to Lisa as if he hugged her just a little bit longer than the others.

"You dudes look great—not like you've been cooped up all winter," he teased them.

"Hey," said Carole indignantly, "we've been riding a lot."

"Why doesn't that surprise me?" John grinned. "Welcome back to the Bar None."

"You know, our parents came this time," Stevie said.

"That's what we heard." Walter nodded.

"They're meeting us here in a few minutes." Lisa looked back toward the bunkhouses. "They're still unpacking."

John smiled at Lisa. "While you're waiting, come and meet my new horse."

Lisa followed John into the barn. She was having trouble keeping a huge grin from spreading across her face.

"His name is Tex," John said. "He's a full-blooded quarter horse with great lines."

They walked to a stall at the far end of the barn. And there was Tex, a beautiful chestnut gelding.

"It's obvious he's got great lines, John," said Lisa. "Pleased to meet you, Tex."

"Likewise, I'm sure," said John in a low voice.

Lisa smiled. John hadn't changed a bit. He was still warm and silly and serious all at the same time. "So tell me everything about him," she said, "like how old is he . . . what's his specialty . . ."

"Well, he's only three and a half, and he has very strong gaits and a sensitive mouth. He was quite well trained, up to a point."

"Which is where *you* come in."

"Exactly," said John. "I think he'd make a super reining horse for wrangling *and* for showing."

"Reining?" Lisa asked, wrinkling her nose. "I don't get it. Don't we all do that?"

John patted Tex and grinned. "Reining is like advanced training for a Western horse. It involves sliding stops, lead changes, pivots. Stuff like that."

"It must take lots of time," said Lisa.

"It has to," said John. "Rushing can really ruin a horse. If you do it right, you have a superior roping horse—and show horse too. Advanced reining with Western quarter horses is the top technical competition."

"It must be useful on the trail and in wrangling too," Lisa said.

John nodded. "That's where it started, after all," he said.

He took her hand as they headed back outside. The parents had gathered already.

Lisa led John over to her parents. "Mom, Dad, this is John Brightstar."

"Pleased to meet you, John," said Mr. Atwood, shaking John's hand. "Are you one of the wranglers here?"

"Well, actually, sir, my dad's the chief wrangler, and I help him before and after school." John turned and introduced the Atwoods to his father.

"Good to meet you," said Walter. "The horses are all saddled up and ready to go. Let's go meet your mounts for the week."

As she and John followed the grown-ups over to the

horses, Lisa wondered if her mother had noticed the two of them holding hands. Mrs. Atwood certainly hadn't shown any reaction.

So far things are going fine, Lisa thought. I just hope I stop feeling so self-conscious around Mom.

"Now, which horse are you going to give me?" Mrs. Atwood was asking Walter. "Do you have a nice, steady one?"

"They're all pretty steady, ma'am," Walter answered, "but I've chosen one of the best for you. You'll be riding Spot."

Spot was a good choice, Lisa thought. He was an Appaloosa gelding that Kate had ridden before she had adopted her mare, Moonglow, from a wild herd. Spot was one of the horses the Bar None used for guests these days. That meant he had to be well trained, reliable, and willing to put up with some less-than-decent riders.

"Spot'll be great for you, Mom," said Lisa as they walked the horse out of the barn. "Now, remember, when you ride Western, you keep the reins much looser than you see us keeping them at Pine Hollow."

Mrs. Atwood gave her daughter a wink. Then she took the reins in her right hand, put her right foot in the right stirrup, and swung herself into the saddle.

Lisa grimaced. "Mom, you mount the horse on the *other* side."

She turned to her father, to start instructing him. But before she could open her mouth, he swung himself up into the saddle from the left side of his horse, Tripper. At least he looked as if he knew what he was doing.

Lisa turned and saw Stevie's parents mounting up. Mr. Lake was riding a mare named Melody. Lisa chuckled to herself. After hearing him sing cowboy songs all day, she thought Melody seemed like the perfect mount. Mrs. Lake was on a gray named Shoofly.

"We'd better hurry up," Stevie joked, "or our parents will leave us in the dust."

As Stevie and Lisa headed back into the barn to collect their own horses, Carole busily adjusted her father's stirrups. "Now, Dad, you don't want your stirrups as short as they are in English riding, and you put your foot a little farther in." She picked up her father's foot and placed it just right in the big wooden stirrup.

"Hold your reins in your right hand. You can loosen up on them, that's ri—"

"Carole, honey, I'm just fine. Now, will you go get your horse?"

Carole looked up at Colonel Hanson and sighed.

There he sat, atop Yellowbird, a big Palomino. He looked okay—except for the hat. On his head was a deluxe Western riding hat, tall and black, with silver buckles around its leather strap, and white and black feathers. The first time she'd laid eyes on it had been on the way to the airport, and she'd wanted to crawl under the backseat of the Lakes' station wagon.

"I still don't know about that hat, Dad," she told him now. "All it needs is a few rhinestones, and you'd look like the dude of the century!"

Colonel Hanson laughed good-naturedly at his daughter. "You're just jealous," he said. "You've got only that old beat-up hat with nothing on it. Now, why don't you go and get your horse and let's get going."

The girls got their horses and mounted up. From previous visits to the Bar None, they each had favorite mounts. Carole always rode Berry, a strawberry roan; Lisa rode a bay mare, Chocolate; and Stevie was on Stewball, a skewbald horse with a lot of personality.

They walked their horses over to a spot just outside the corral, where their parents were waiting.

Mr. Lake spoke up. "You know, you don't need to pamper us, girls. We haven't watched all those shows and lessons at Pine Hollow without picking up a thing or two."

"We're not as run-down as you think we are," Carole's father added with a wink at his daughter.

Mrs. Atwood adjusted her hat. "You're treating us like a bunch of old bags!"

"That's right," chimed in Stevie's mother. "And if we're bags, we must really be *saddlebags*!"

Everybody laughed.

"Our very own nickname," said Mrs. Atwood. "Maybe we should start our own club!"

The parents chuckled, the kids groaned, and they all started off.

The girls and John took the parents on an easy trail ride along a few of the Bar None's hundreds of acres. They led them out beyond the compound of buildings and into the open fields that sprawled behind the ranch. All around them, huge, snowcapped peaks jutted into the sky. The pastures were lined with grass and scrub and small trees here and there. At their edges, pine forests created a layer of dark green.

There was no other trail-riding like this in the world, Lisa thought. It was beautiful here.

They walked at first, so their parents could enjoy the

view. Then Carole looked back and assessed that everyone looked pretty comfortable, so she brought Berry to a slow trot.

Lisa watched to see what her parents would do. Sure enough, her mother brought her feet about a foot away from Spot's sides and then let them bang against him with a smack of a kick. The horse arched his neck and started to lope. But he was a trail horse, used to following the leader, so he quickly slowed to a trot.

It's a good thing Spot's a follower, thought Lisa. Otherwise, with a kick like that, he'd be off to the other side of the mountain.

Mrs. Atwood had lost her stirrups by this time and was bouncing precariously in the saddle. "Whoa, whoa," she said as she pulled hard on the reins.

"Mom," said Lisa, circling around and coming up beside her mother, "let's stop and regroup."

Lisa stopped Chocolate. Spot stopped also.

"Whew," said Mrs. Atwood as she fumbled for the stirrups with her feet. "Aren't these stirrups a bit long?"

"They're just right for Western riding, Mom," answered Lisa. "Try to keep your feet pressed into them. And you don't need to kick so hard. A little squeeze will do."

"I see." Mrs. Atwood found her stirrups. Without another word to her daughter, she clucked to Spot, who broke into a trot, following the others. Lisa trotted along as well, keeping a close eye on her mother.

As the group approached the hills where Parson's Rock jutted up out of the land, Carole slowed them back down to a walk.

"That's the rock I told you about," Stevie said to her parents. "Remember the surprise birthday party my friends gave me on my very first visit out here? That's where they held it." They stopped to admire the huge rock that stood up out of the hills like a preacher's pulpit.

Then the group wound up into the hills a little way before heading back to the Bar None. Kate led the riders back. John rode beside Lisa, who checked on her mother every few minutes.

Carole rode up beside her father, who was swaying quite a bit in the saddle. "You don't have to sway so much, Dad," she said.

He tilted his hat toward her until it looked like it would fall off. Carole shook her head and rode up to take the lead with Kate. Her father wasn't about to take this trail ride seriously.

Soon they were back at the corral.

"That was great!" Stevie's father said as he dismounted. "I'll take trail-riding in the Rockies over golf in Virginia any day. And Melody," he said to his horse, "you're the best durn, rough-ridin' pony this cowboy's ever seen." And with that Mr. Lake gave his horse a slap on the rump. Which she took as a signal to move forward. She started toward the barn.

"Whoa, not so fast, little lady," said Mr. Lake, grabbing at the reins.

"Dad," said Stevie, "you aren't supposed to smack a horse that hard on the rump unless you want her to *go* somewhere."

"Sorry, girl," said Mr. Lake to his horse. This time he gently patted Melody on the neck.

"I thought that ride was a piece of cake!" said Colonel Hanson.

"I love these views," added Mrs. Lake. "Every single place you look, the scenery's incredible!"

At that moment the big triangle that hung on the ranch-house porch was rung loud and long.

"You think the views are great, Mom," said Stevie, "wait till you taste the food!"

\*       \*       \*

33

LISA'S FATHER PILED his plate high with fried chicken and coleslaw at dinner. He glanced at Phyllis Devine. "My compliments to the chef. It looks like the food you serve is one of the secrets to the ranch's great success!"

Colonel Hanson raised his glass of iced tea. "Hear, hear!"

Everyone lifted their glasses to Phyllis, and then they all dug in.

Lisa noticed that even her mother was enjoying dinner. Instead of her perpetual diet of salad, Mrs. Atwood had actually put a drumstick and a roll on her plate.

After the last slices of pie were eaten and the last plates and glasses cleared from the table, the parents and daughters teamed up for a quick game of charades.

For the last round, Mr. Lake stepped up and opened his mouth, but no sound came out. He had one hand on his chest, and he wiggled his Adam's apple with the other hand.

"Song titles!" Lisa yelled.

Mr. Lake nodded.

"Figures," said Stevie. They all burst out laughing as Mr. Lake frowned at his daughter, then began waving his hands and flapping his arms.

"Wings!" Carole called.

" 'On the Wings of Love,' " Stevie shouted.

Mr. Lake shook his head and flapped harder.

" 'Wind Beneath My Wings!' " Lisa guessed it. And they all collapsed in giggles.

"You're much better when you're not making any noise, Dad," Stevie teased.

Mr. Lake yawned. "I guess that's my cue . . . to turn in, and save the rest of the songs for tomorrow."

THE GIRLS WERE in their pj's, going over the events of the day.

"I think my mom ended up enjoying the trail ride," said Lisa. "She had a rough patch when she practically kicked a hole in Spot's sides, but thanks to Spot's good temper, she finally started getting the hang of it."

"It's fun to see my parents having such a good time," said Stevie. "I just wish my dad wouldn't try to show off. Did you see when he whacked Melody on the rump? She almost flew right up to the weather vane on the barn roof!"

Carole rolled her eyes.

"Did you notice my dad, with his feet sticking way out in front of him? He was rocking from side to side so much, I thought Yellowbird might get dizzy! And when I said something about it, he just laughed it off, like it was some big joke."

"I know what you mean," said Lisa. "My mom certainly doesn't like me telling her what to do either."

"I wish they would take the whole thing more seriously," Carole went on. "Just because *we're* the ones giving them suggestions on how to be better riders doesn't mean they shouldn't try and do what we say."

"They're acting like the kids," said Lisa.

"Right!" Carole agreed. For her, good horsemanship came above everything else, and she had very high standards.

The problem was the Saddlebags didn't see things quite the same way.

LISA GULPED THE last of her hot chocolate and looked at Stevie, who was digging into thirds on French toast. "Come on," she said.

Stevie nodded, but kept on eating.

"Steeeevie," Lisa persisted, "are you going to eat or ride?"

"Vofe!" Stevie answered.

"What?"

Stevie chewed and swallowed. "Both."

"Wellll . . ."

"I know where *you* want to go," said Stevie. "I heard

Kate say John's out in the corral, working with his new horse."

"Well, wouldn't you rather watch him and *learn* something than eat?"

"Sometimes," said Stevie as she put her napkin on the table and stood up. "But with food like this, it's debatable."

Kate met the girls on their way out the door. "I was just coming in to get you guys. You've got to see this. John and Tex, they're amazing!"

"We know, we know," said Stevie, elbowing Lisa in the ribs.

The three girls headed out to the corral, where they joined Carole, who had climbed atop the post-and-rail fence to get a better view.

"Even though Tex came to us perfectly trained at walk, trot, lope, and gallop," Kate said, "the stuff he and John are doing now is new for both of them. Reining is kind of like dressage, but it looks more like the fancy moves cowboys used to do in all those old Westerns."

"What do you call that halt he's practicing now?" asked Lisa.

"A sliding stop. Right now he's practicing it out of a walk. But he'll be up to a gallop soon."

John looked over at the girls and waved. He walked Tex to the far end of the corral, turned him down the center, and brought him to a trot. Then, with a soft "Whoa," John lifted the reins and sat back deep in the saddle. Tex stopped short, bringing his hindquarters beneath him.

"Good boy." John walked him to the near end of the corral and turned him to try it again.

"The secret of learning all these moves," Kate went on, "is to start slow. That way, John teaches Tex the response at a walk and trot, and doesn't have to pull hard on his mouth when he stops from a faster gait. Watch what he does now."

Lisa kept her eyes on John as he brought Tex to a lope. When he was practically at the end of the corral, he signaled the horse. Tex's hind feet slid under him. His weight was on his rear haunches and his forelegs just left the ground. But he kept his balance perfectly and in another instant he stood up, balanced on all four legs.

Carole let out a low whistle. "That was great."

"Now watch this," said Kate as John walked to one end of the corral and started backing Tex up. "Looks like normal dressage backing, right?"

"Yeah, it does," said Lisa.

"Just watch," said Kate.

John slowly and patiently backed Tex up one, two, three, four, five, six, seven paces and kept on going.

"He's backing him practically the whole length of the ring!" Stevie said in awe.

"In a Western reining show class, sometimes that's what you have to do," Kate explained.

When John and Tex reached the far end of the corral, the four girls burst into applause. John tipped his hat and trotted toward them. "You don't know how long it took us to get that right," he said.

"I believe it," said Carole.

Lisa was speechless, just grinning at John.

"Now I've got to work on these pivots." John rode to the fence opposite them.

"A pivot is different in a reining class than in a dressage class," Kate explained. "You'll see right away."

John brought Tex to a lope at the far end of the corral, parallel to the fence.

"He's really close to the fence, isn't he?" said Stevie.

A second later she gasped. John had stopped Tex on a dime. Tex pushed off with his right foreleg, reared up a bit, turned ninety degrees, and landed—facing the girls.

Finally John rode over to his audience.

"You were great!" Lisa beamed.

"You two really look like you know what you're doing," said Kate.

John patted Tex's neck. "Thanks. Tex and I'll be entering some shows in a few months, and I guess if we work every day—"

"You'll be ready," Carole finished for him.

"She's right, John," Kate added. "And Carole ought to know. She's ridden in some pretty tough shows."

Carole blushed and glanced at her watch. "Do you think these lazy parents of ours are still asleep?"

"Nope," came Walter's deep voice. "They've been up longer than you. I put them all on their horses at seven-thirty this morning."

"What?" Stevie blanched. "All five of them?"

"All five," Walter confirmed. "Carole, your dad said they'd have no problem. Said he's a volunteer at your Pony Club. Seems he knows the ropes."

"*Seems* is right." Carole hopped down from the fence. "He doesn't have a clue."

"Neither do any of the others!" Stevie practically shouted.

Walter stared at the girls with a lopsided grin. "I've watched your folks ride. I'm sure they'll be okay."

Lisa shook her head. "You don't know our parents, Walter. They don't understand that riding is serious business—not just fun."

"We'd better go find them," said Carole.

Walter shrugged. "If that's what you want to do."

As the girls headed toward the barn to collect their horses, Walter called after them. "I gave your parents directions for the little loop. They headed north first, then they ought to turn east at the edge of the first field, ride to the end of it, and head back south by southwest."

"Gotcha," called Kate. The foursome saddled up their horses, mounted quickly, then headed out. Kate led the girls along the path Walter had mapped out, only she started at the end and went in the opposite direction.

"If we go this way, we can head them off," Lisa commented, realizing what Kate was up to. "I hope they're okay."

They started trotting.

"They've been gone over two hours on a ride that should take less than one," said Stevie.

"Could they have gotten lost?" Lisa asked.

"What if one of them fell?" Carole bit her lip. "And got badly hurt?"

They broke into a lope, then a gallop.

42

But there was no sign of the parents.

Kate slowed Moonglow. "If your folks are off the trail, we may miss them," she said. "Let's trot for a while." The others followed.

Stevie gazed around at the desert brush.

"Are there rattlers during this time of year?"

"There are always rattlers," Kate said.

This time they all panned the landscape.

The first sign of parents that Stevie saw was Colonel Hanson's black ten-gallon hat on top his head. The five parents were riding out of a patch of woods and heading toward them. Mrs. Lake, on Shoofly, was directly behind the colonel, ambling along. Stevie's father was behind her, and as they approached, Stevie could hear him serenading the group with "Red River Valley."

"I can't believe it," said Stevie. "They get us really worried and here they are, moseying along, singing 'Red River Valley.' Couldn't you just scream?"

The girls trotted up to their parents.

"Where have you been?" asked Carole. "We were so worried!"

The parents exchanged a chuckle.

"You were worried about us?" Mr. Atwood said.

"Did you stick to the trail Walter mapped out?" Stevie demanded.

"What's the matter, don't you trust us?" Mr. Lake shook his head at his daughter. "Of course we stuck to the trail."

"And what if we didn't?" said Mrs. Atwood.

Lisa shook her head. "Mom, have you ever heard of rattlers?"

"You girls are overreacting!" Mrs. Atwood responded. "You saw how well we did yesterday, and we did just as well today. I'll have you know . . ."

As she spoke, Mrs. Atwood yanked on Spot's reins. He kept pulling back, yawning with his mouth and trying to get the bit out of his way.

"Mom!" said Lisa. "*Pleeease* loosen up on your reins. If you knew what you were doing, you wouldn't be handling Spot that way."

"Young lady," Mrs. Atwood began sharply, "I really don't think you should speak to me like that."

Lisa noticed her mother did loosen up on the reins, though.

"Sorry, Mom," said Lisa, sighing with relief.

Carole and Berry had ridden up next to Lisa. When Mrs. Atwood wasn't looking, Carole shot Lisa a secret smile. Lisa knew Carole was proud of her for giving her mother some instructions—even if it did mean risking her mother's anger.

"Let's go back," Lisa said. She and Carole turned and led the group back the way the girls had come.

5

AT LUNCHTIME THE next day, after everyone had gathered around the table, Frank Devine cleared his throat. "I have some exciting news for everyone."

Everyone turned toward him. Exciting news? thought Lisa. What could it be?

"We have to move our cattle back to the south pasture," he continued. "Right now they're all over in one of the far northwestern ones."

Stevie punched the air. "Yaaahoooo! A cattle drive!"

"Right you are, Stevie," answered Frank with a wide

grin. "I thought it'd be fun for everybody to come along."

"Including us Saddlebags?" Stevie's mother asked.

"Of course," Frank replied.

"Oh, that *does* sound like fun," said Mrs. Atwood.

Carole looked around the table pensively. Fun? She wasn't so sure. She loved cattle drives, but they usually involved lots of hard work. Would the Saddlebags really be up to it? She tapped nervously on her water glass.

Stevie and Lisa had grown quiet too. Carole could tell they were having similar thoughts.

When the meal was finished, Stevie cut herself some apple pie and sat next to Carole.

Colonel Hanson turned to his daughter. "You're quiet, honey. Don't you have faith in us?"

"Well, Dad, it's just that cattle drives aren't as easy as they look in the movies. You're in the saddle the whole day long, and sometimes things can happen—"

"Carole, dear, you know we're getting the hang of it," Mr. Lake said.

"We might be the Saddlebags, and we might not be ready to rope a little dogie and stay on our horse at the same time," said Mrs. Lake, "but I'm game."

"What's a little dogie anyway?" asked Mr. Atwood. "Isn't it some kind of submarine sandwich?"

"Daaaad!" said Lisa, turning red over her father's pun on hoagies, which was what such sandwiches were called in some places. "A little dogie is a motherless calf! Sometimes they get separated from the herd on the drive and you have to rescue them."

"I could do that," said her mother. "I bet they're cute."

"They are," Lisa answered, shaking her head. "But it's not that simple." She paused to take a deep breath. "You know how Max is always telling us that riding is fun, but it's serious too?"

"Mmmhm," answered Mr. Atwood.

"Well, I just think you need to be aware that it can get *very* serious sometimes."

"We take it seriously enough," said Mrs. Lake, waving one hand dismissively. "Frankly, I don't see why you girls are getting so nervous. You're being the party poopers around here, not us. I can't *wait* to sleep under the stars. . . ."

"And listen to my serenade," said Mr. Lake. " 'I'm a headin' for my first roundup!' "

Frank rose from his chair. "You'll all be fine. You girls

can keep your parents in line. Now it's siesta time. I'll see everyone later."

THE GIRLS TOOK to their bunkhouse for the next hour. Their siesta time would be perfect for a much-needed Saddle Club meeting.

Stevie stretched out on her top bunk and looked up at the beams in the roof. "Hmph," she said. "Frank thinks they'll be okay."

"And that we can keep them in line," added Lisa grimly. "I bet they'll be harder to handle than those stray dogies." She groaned. "Speaking of dogies—did you hear my father making that dumb joke about submarine sandwiches? That was classic!"

Kate giggled. "He's just showing his dude colors."

Lisa groaned again.

"I don't know about you guys," said Carole as she took off her boots and stretched out on her bunk, "but I thought my dad looked worse than ever on the ride this morning. He sways back and forth with Yellowbird's gait, and the hat bounces left and right and it makes *me* dizzy! Either the hat's going to fall off his head or he's going to fall out from under the hat. I don't know which'll happen first!"

"I think if my dad bursts into song one more time," Stevie chimed in, "I may take *my* hat off and send it sailing straight at him."

"And my mom's riding is making me sick," Lisa said. "I mean, how could she be *my* mom? Maybe, once upon a time, she had a riding lesson. But if she did, it was at the yank-and-kick school of riding."

"Look, guys," said Kate, "tons of the guests who come here are rank beginners. A lot of them know even *less* than your parents do—and they manage just fine. The only ones who really give us trouble are the people who think they can do more than they actually can. That can lead to danger."

"That's just it," said Carole. "I think—I *know*—my dad thinks he's *much* more capable than he really is."

"Same with my parents," Stevie declared.

Lisa said, "Mine too."

"I'll tell you what," Kate suggested. "Why don't we invite all the parents to join us tomorrow morning before the cattle drive, while we watch John train with Tex?"

"Good idea," said Lisa, quickly catching on to Kate's idea. "Then they'll see how much technique it takes to be an excellent rider, and it'll be fresh in their minds for the ride."

"Where exactly will the cattle drive take us?" Stevie asked.

"Dad made it sound farther than it is," Kate told her. "It'll take us only a few hours to ride to the pasture northwest of here, where the herd is. Then we'll sleep out. Next morning we'll bring the herd to the back pasture near the ranch. It's a cinch of a ride, and the herd's not that big this time."

"So it's really a one-day drive that Walter and John could handle without any help from any of us dudes, young *or* old," Stevie remarked.

"Well, that's how we run the ranch," answered Kate. "Guests come on a simple drive and get the feel and the thrill of riding the herd, sleeping under the stars, cooking out. You know. This same drive has been done by guests with less experience than the Saddlebags. What could possibly go wrong?"

"Nothing, I guess," said Lisa.

"I'll never forget what went wrong for me on my first drive," said Stevie. "Remember the rattlesnake, and poor Tomahawk?"

"Do I ever," Carole answered with a shudder. She

would never forget the day Stevie had fallen off a horse and come face-to-face with a rattler. Now it was a grim reminder of how dangerous riding without experience could be. "Our parents are definitely not prepared for the worst that could happen."

"I guess we just have to hope for the best," said Stevie, "an uneventful ride, clear skies—"

"And Saddlebags who understand how much hard work is involved," Lisa interrupted.

THE NEXT MORNING the girls led their parents to the corral just as John Brightstar was swinging into the saddle.

"What he's training for is something called reining," Kate explained, "and it's good for developing a superior wrangling horse, but also for shows." She hiked herself on top of the fence. "Now watch John carefully," she continued, "he's going to warm up by practicing all four gaits with Tex: walk, trot, lope—which is like a canter in English riding—and gallop, or run. This is to make sure that Tex and he are perfectly balanced at all speeds, because balance is going to matter a lot later."

Lisa glanced at her mother. Her eyes were glazed over, as if she were still half asleep or just not interested in what Kate was saying.

John trotted to the center of the ring, halted, and started backing up.

"That's harder than it looks," said Kate, "and making it look easy is one of the most important things John's teaching Tex. John has to lean forward a bit in the saddle, and still press his seat down. He also must pull with the reins just enough to give the signal to back up, but not so much that the horse starts to have what they call a yawning mouth."

Stevie looked over and saw her father stifle a huge yawn. Lisa saw it too.

"Take a look at *that* yawning mouth!" Stevie whispered to Lisa. They both covered their mouths to keep from laughing aloud.

"Now, the reason why this is difficult," Kate went on, oblivious to the lack of attention she was getting, "is that the rider uses neck reining to pivot the horse. He doesn't pull on the mouth at all."

"Does Stewball know how to do this stuff?" Stevie asked Kate.

"Sure," Kate answered. "That's why he's such a good roping horse."

"Can I try?" Stevie asked.

"Sure."

Stevie jumped down from the fence and walked into the barn.

Lisa shook her head in admiration of her friend. Stevie was always ready to take on a new horseback-riding challenge, no matter how difficult it looked. She had mastered some tough dressage routines for events back home; now nothing could stop her from trying this new skill. Lisa hopped down from the fence and followed Stevie and Kate into the barn.

Carole looked around at the parents. Mrs. Atwood had wandered over to the garden, and Mrs. Lake was busily drawing a tic-tac-toe board in the dirt with her toe. Meanwhile her father was looking at some all-terrain vehicles parked in the driveway. Only Mr. Atwood and Mr. Lake remained nearby. "We're going to try our hands at some of this stuff," Carole told the two fathers. "Any of you guys up for a turn?"

"No, thanks," said Mr. Atwood, "I think I'll save my energy for the real thing."

Mr. Lake shook his head no.

So much for Kate's plan to impress the parents with our skills, thought Carole.

Just then Stevie rode Stewball almost all the way down the corral. She tightened the reins and sat even deeper in her seat. Immediately the horse slid his rear haunches beneath him into sort of a half kneel, and let his front legs rise off the ground for about two seconds, before coming to a full balanced stance.

"Whoowee!" Stevie shouted. She looked around for her parents. But they were just heading back into the ranch house, not the least bit interested in their daughter's reining technique.

"Way to go, Stevie," Carole called.

Oh, well, Stevie thought. At least my friends are impressed.

LATER, AFTER THE GIRLS had practiced backing, pivots, and sliding stops, they unsaddled and watered their horses.

"That was great backing, Lisa," said Kate. "I've never seen Chocolate do so well."

"Thanks," Lisa answered. "I learned a lot from watching John, but I'm not sure how much the Saddlebags learned."

"They didn't pay the least bit attention," said Carole. "It's too bad. A lot of those skills are essential on a drive."

"I guess our plan didn't exactly work," said Kate.

"Nope." Stevie looked glum. "My mother didn't even notice how much work John's done with his horse. She was too busy playing tic-tac-toe."

"Well, at least we appreciate him," Kate pointed out. "You have to remember that not everyone is as horse crazy as the members of The Saddle Club."

"That's for sure," Carole agreed. "Come on, let's get some lunch before the cattle drive starts."

STEVIE POKED HER head into her parents' bunkhouse. "How's the packing coming?" she asked.

Her mother was busy laying out her bedroll: sleeping bag, change of clothes, toiletries, and a big hardcover book.

"Oh, Mom, don't bring the book! It's much too heavy!"

Mr. and Mrs. Lake both started to chuckle.

"Aw, c'mon, sweetie, we've been on camping trips before!" Mrs. Lake said, rolling her eyes.

"But this one's on a *horse*! You don't do a bedroll like

*that*." Stevie went to her mother and took over the job. "Where's your towel? It should be in here too. And tomorrow's socks are missing!"

"Whoa!" Mr. Lake exclaimed. "Since when did you get so darn organized?"

Stevie made a face at her father. "It's a trail ride, Dad! You don't want your socks falling out on the trail while you're loping along behind some steer. And you don't need that super-duper heavy-duty flashlight!" She went over to his bedroll and took out the four-battery flashlight he was trying to roll up into it. "Just pack the small one you brought."

"Okay, okay. You're the expert, little miss."

"*Hmph!*" said Stevie, and continued helping them with their rolls. "Give me your ponchos. These are essential. They go on the outside, for easy access."

Mrs. Lake stood with her hands on her hips, grinning at her daughter. "Stevie, you never fail to surprise me. Around home you're not exactly organized, but when it comes to packing for a trail ride, you are truly an expert." She went over and gave Stevie a quick hug. "Actually, I don't know what we'd do without you."

\*     \*     \*

CAROLE WENT TO the main house to check on her father's packing. "Have you remembered all the essentials?" she asked.

Colonel Hanson looked up from his packing and put his hands on his hips. "My flaky daughter is trying to organize *me*? Have you forgotten what I do for a living?"

"Well, Dad, when you're going on a cattle drive, you can't be forgetful," Carole answered, blushing a little. "What about that toothbrush—did you remember it?"

"Are you worried about me by any odd chance?" Colonel Hanson went over and gave his daughter a hug. "Don't be."

"Okay," she agreed. "I'll stop. But only after I make sure you've got your poncho."

LISA PULLED A blow-dryer out of her mother's bedroll. "Mom," she said, "first of all, we're going to be sleeping outside, remember? There's no electricity. Second, there are no showers where we're going, just a creek."

Mrs. Atwood looked sheepish. "Oh, of course," she said.

Lisa put the blow-dryer back in the bathroom. "Let's leave this here."

"I guess I'll just bring a scarf for my hair for the second day," said Mrs. Atwood.

"Good idea," answered Lisa, moving to check on her father's bedroll. Who knew what he had packed?

THAT AFTERNOON ALL the cattle-drive riders assembled outside the barn. Walter and John had already tacked up their own mounts and strapped on bedrolls and equipment.

"Your horses have all been cut," said Walter. "Time to saddle up and secure your bedrolls."

Carole and Kate were the first to tack up. Once their horses were ready, they turned to help the parents.

John smiled at Lisa as he helped her tighten the bedroll on the back of Chocolate's saddle. "This'll be a fun ride," he said.

"If my mom can learn how to do things for herself," Lisa muttered under her breath as she watched her mother struggle to adjust her stirrups, then ask Kate for help.

Finally all riders were ready, all horses saddled up, all bedrolls fastened on.

"Let's ride out," said Walter.

Lisa swung herself into the saddle and led the way beside John and Tex. Mr. and Mrs. Atwood followed.

"Well, pa'dnah, looks lak wee're finely off!" Mr. Atwood called out.

Lisa cringed. "I'm not related to the man who said that," she murmured.

"They're dudes—what do you expect?" John said softly.

Lisa grinned in spite of herself. "You're right," she said. She was glad to be riding with John—even if her parents *were* dudes. If he didn't mind, why should she?

Stevie and Carole fell into line behind their parents, with Walter bringing up the rear behind them.

"Wait till my father launches into his favorite cowboy—" Stevie began.

" 'As I was out walking the streets of Laredo . . . ,' " Mr. Lake started in at the top of his lungs as if on cue.

When he finished the verse, he took off his hat, waved it in the air, and said, "Go west, young man! I mean, young woman! I mean, young people!"

Colonel Hanson looked back at him and said, "Hey, what about this one, 'Whoopee-ti-yi-yo, git along, little dogies . . .' "

"Oh, well." Carole sighed. "At least they're *all* making fools of themselves."

"True," said Stevie. There was no way she'd argue with that.

SOON THE COWBOY songs tapered off, and the riders grew quiet. Lisa gazed at the scene spread out in front of her. In the distance rose the jagged, snow-covered peaks of the Rockies. Before her was an enormous stretch of flat grazing fields. How could pastures get this big? Lisa wondered. Back in Virginia, meadows and grazing fields seemed tiny compared to this.

Suddenly Lisa remembered her parents, and felt glad to be sharing this scene with them. She turned around, and sure enough, her mother looked awed as she took in the incredible scenery and pointed out different things to Mr. Atwood.

As the riders reached the end of one stretch of grazing land, the trail turned slightly to the north, following the base of a small hill. John and Lisa brought their horses to a trot as they rounded the hill, and the others followed.

John and Tex slowed to a walk as the land started sloping downward. It became dry and rocky.

"We have to cross this creek bed, or arroyo, as they

call it," John explained, "so that we can ride up on the herd at the right angle."

Lisa followed, motioning over her shoulder for the rest of the group to come along. The ground underfoot was covered with large rocks and small stones and pebbles. "Take it slow," she called to those behind her.

The horses carefully picked their way across the stony, dry creek bed.

At the very bottom of the arroyo, a tiny stream of water flowed through. John stopped and let Tex stretch his head down to drink the cool water. "We'll stop here tomorrow on the way back too, to water the cattle."

All the riders followed suit, stopping to let their horses have a drink. Then John and Lisa led the group in a trot to the far northwest grazing lands.

Lisa felt much better about her parents' riding than she had yesterday, or even that morning. That afternoon they'd seemed impressed by the landscape and followed John's instructions without a single problem or joke. She looked back, and gave a thumbs-up to Stevie.

Stevie returned the signal, flashing Lisa a huge grin. Obviously Stevie felt relieved too.

So far so good, Lisa thought.

Just as the sun began lowering into the west, the group from the Bar None reached the top of a little ridge. Below them, the herd of cattle stood grazing peacefully in the late afternoon sun. The riders lined up at the edge of the hill and silently watched the scene.

Mr. Lake broke the silence, crooning, " 'Oh give me a home, where the holsteins roam—' "

"Dad," Stevie interrupted, "you're getting so predictable!"

"Okay," he said, "how about this one, 'From this valley they say you are going—' "

"All right, let's start down," John interrupted.

Riders and horses reached the campsite as the sun met the western horizon.

Everyone dismounted, unsaddled their horses, and followed John and Walter's lead, laying the saddles out in a line.

John and Lisa took the food and equipment packs over to the open fireplace. Carole, Kate, and Stevie stayed to help Walter water and feed the horses.

Carole pulled a hoof pick out of her pocket and started checking all the horses' hooves for stones, one by one. She looked up from her work and noticed the parents milling around near the campsite.

"It's a good thing for these tired horses that someone knows horse care around here," she said, digging dirt and stones out of Yellowbird's hoof.

Stevie set down the two water buckets she was carrying. "And I'm sure all this work would go a lot faster if *everyone* helped out," she put in with a pointed look in the parents' direction.

When Stevie was returning from the creek with her eighth serving of water, she looked up to see her father coming their way. True to form, he was whistling a cowboy tune.

"Did you ever think of a career in country music instead of law?" she asked.

"How about as a cowpoke?" was his answer. "Whatchou pardners doin' over heyar?"

"C'mon, Dad, every cowboy knows horse care is no joke," answered his daughter. "No rest until these horses are completely taken care of. That's Max's rule too. Horse care before people care."

"Need any help?"

"Sure," Stevie answered, handing him two buckets. "Works better if you fill them two at a time," she said.

"Got it, pardner," he replied.

After the horses were watered and fed, Carole picked up a brush and handed it to Stevie's father. "The last thing to do is brush some of this trail dust off the horses."

"Brush with the hairline," instructed Stevie, "and, most important, the saddle area and the legs. Here's a sponge and scraper for the really sweaty places."

"What about water?" asked Mr. Lake.

"There's a bucket," Stevie said, pointing. "And there's the stream."

Mr. Lake helped the girls until the last horse was watered, fed, cleaned up, and content. Then he took

Stevie's hand and they walked over to the campsite together. She was happy he'd realized it was time for everyone to pitch in, no matter how tired the riders were. In fact, she was so pleased, she almost started whistling "The Streets of Laredo" herself.

OVER BY THE fireplace, which was actually a small circle of rocks on the ground, Lisa and John were hard at work.

Together they had gathered wood, laid the fire, and lit it. John pulled a folded metal grill from one of the packs. Then they moved stones around so the grill would fit securely on top of the fire.

John stood up and surveyed their handiwork. "Looks like it'll be hot enough soon."

"I didn't realize how starving I was till just now," Lisa answered. As she turned to get the food out of the pack, her mother walked up.

"How's everything coming along?" she asked.

"The fire's almost ready for grilling," answered Lisa. "Would you like to help make supper?"

"Sure," said Mrs. Atwood, "just put me to work."

The three of them formed a cookout assembly line. Lisa took out hot dogs and prepared hamburgers for the grill, while John stood over the fire, cooking the meat.

Mrs. Atwood prepared plates with buns and rolls, then took the food when it was ready and added relish and ketchup.

"Chow time!" Mrs. Atwood called. Then she passed around the first few plates of freshly grilled supper.

Lisa was the last one to sit down and eat. Hungrily, she took a bite of hamburger. Mmm, she thought. Nothing tastes better than campfire food.

It was also nice to see that her mother had figured out there was more to ranch life than kick-and-yank riding, and always being waited on.

After she finished eating, Lisa checked the food pack again. "Save room for dessert!" she called. And she took out of the pack a box of chocolate bars, a box of graham crackers, and some rather crushed marshmallows.

"S'mores!" Stevie shouted. "Everybody get a roasting stick!"

This time even the parents moved quickly. No one wanted to miss out on the delicious campfire treats.

AFTER S'MORES THE group began telling ghost stories. Lisa watched John as he got up and silently started clearing the tin plates and cups. She wondered if he had volunteered for cleanup so he wouldn't have to take a turn at

68

storytelling. But she knew he was a good storyteller—she'd heard him before. Maybe he felt a little shy around the grown-ups. She stood and began picking up the remaining dishes.

John had put the plates and cups in a bucket and taken them down to the creek. There he filled the bucket with water and soap and started washing dishes.

"I brought you a few little dogies," said Lisa as she walked up with a stack of dirty dishes.

John smiled. "Perfect timing." He put the dishes in the bucket and pointed to a towel hanging on the twig of a nearby tree. "You can rinse them in the stream and then dry, if you like."

Lisa took the towel and started rinsing and drying plates and silverware. "I've really had fun watching you work on Tex," she said. "I can't believe those sliding stops. I mean, it looks as though he's going to do a somersault, and he keeps his balance so perfectly. And so do you. You guys look great!"

John kept his eyes on the dishes. "Thanks," he said.

"When do you get a chance to do the work?" Lisa asked.

John looked up at her. "Actually, I get up around five every morning—"

*"Five?"*

He nodded. "And I do barn chores, then work with Tex for an hour before school. Then we work again when I get home."

"Yikes! It must be fun though."

"It is."

"With riding—there's always more than enough to learn, even for an excellent rider," Lisa said thoughtfully. "I'm not sure some people get that."

"Like who?"

"Like our parents," she said with a sigh.

He came over to her and gave her shoulders a squeeze. "Your parents are really no different from most of the dudes who come here on vacation. They enjoy being at the Bar None, and get into it, but they don't really get what it's all about. At least your folks are having a good time."

Lisa thought about what he said. John had a better perspective on her parents than she did, she realized. "Thanks," she told him. "I guess I'm just embarrassed or something."

John kept his arm around her shoulders. "Anyway," he said, "I'm glad you're here."

Lisa swallowed hard. She couldn't think of what to say next.

They were silent for a while, listening to the sound of the horses munching on the scrub grass nearby, and the soft lowing of the cattle in the distance. In the sky over their heads, millions of stars twinkled, and the Milky Way was a wash of soft white.

As Lisa stared upward, John gently brought his hand to her face and turned her toward him. He brushed his lips against hers.

*Crunch crunch crunch.*

Footsteps, coming closer. John and Lisa pulled back from each other and turned toward the sound.

Lisa couldn't believe her eyes. It was her mother.

MRS. ATWOOD WALKED up to John and Lisa and put her hands on her hips. "So. I guess you two are on cleanup crew."

Lisa could feel her face turning beet red. She couldn't tell if her mother was angry, or embarrassed, or both. At that moment all Lisa wanted was for the ground to open beneath her feet and swallow her up.

"Uh, Mom," squeaked Lisa, "could you take this stack of clean plates?"

Mrs. Atwood picked up a load of clean dishes. So did Lisa and John. As they headed back to the campsite,

Mrs. Atwood turned to John and said, "What's your name again?"

Lisa stumbled over a root and fell down headfirst, scattering the tin plates everywhere.

Her mother helped her to her feet. "Let me just take these dishes back to the campsite, and I'll come back and help you with the others."

Lisa watched her go, then bent down to pick up the plates. As John leaned over to help her, they both started giggling. Pretty soon, Lisa and John were doubled over in giggles, and having trouble holding on to the plates they were picking up. Luckily, Mrs. Atwood didn't come back to help out.

When they finally returned to the campsite, story time was just breaking up.

"Any dishes left for me to do?" asked Mrs. Atwood.

"No," said Lisa, avoiding her mother's eyes. "But there'll be other chances tomorrow."

She headed for her bedroll. John gave her a silent wave. And from under his shock of black bangs she thought she saw him flash a quick wink.

She laid out her bedroll between the sleeping bags of her two best friends. She opened it up and took out her toothbrush.

"Coming with me to the washhouse under the stars?" Stevie asked.

"Sure am," said Lisa. They walked back to the creek to brush their teeth.

"You'll never guess what happened," said Lisa to Stevie under her breath.

"Does it have anything to do with your mom's showing up at the creek?" Stevie asked.

Lisa nodded. "John was about to kiss me, when my mom walked up."

Stevie gasped. "You must've been soooo embarrassed!" she said. "I remember once, when Phil had walked me home and was kissing me good-bye, Chad opened up the front door! I wanted to absolutely disappear right then and there!"

"Yup," Lisa agreed. "I wanted the exact same thing. But instead, I scattered clean dishes all over the ground!"

"How dramatic!" Stevie said, and they both burst out laughing.

After they'd gone to check the horses one last time, The Saddle Club members headed back to their section of the campsite. They all used their old technique of putting tomorrow's clean socks and underwear in the bottom of their sleeping bags. That way, when morning came, they could change into their already warm clean clothes right inside their sleeping bags.

Stevie kissed her parents good night. "Do me a favor, Dad," she said.

"What's that, honey?"

"Please! No singing before breakfast!" Stevie gave him and her mother a hug and scooted back to The Saddle Club's row of bedrolls.

Carole went over to say good night to her father. He was straightening out his bedroll, his ten-gallon hat still on his head.

"Are you going to sleep with that hat on?" Carole asked him.

"Not sure, not sure," was his answer. "See you in the morning, hon."

"Good night, Dad."

"Night, Mom. Night, Dad," said Lisa softly as she gave each of her parents a kiss.

Kate was already tucked in her bedroll when the other three girls came back.

"I thought we were going to have a quick meeting of The Saddle Club," said Stevie, "to sort of wrap up the day."

"Jaddadh wheep . . . ," Kate attempted to say.

Lisa grinned. "I think that translates into 'Gotta sleep.' And I for one second the motion."

"Okay, okay," Stevie agreed, and the four girls snuggled deep down in their bedrolls.

Lisa couldn't believe how far they were from Willow Creek. She'd been on overnight trail rides back east, but they never felt like these cattle drives did. She looked up and started counting stars.

One, two, three . . . She listened to the cattle lowing in the near distance. She felt surrounded by huge, expansive warmth. The earth beneath her, the stars like a big high blanket, the hum of the hundreds of cattle in her ears. Nine, ten, eleven . . . By the time she'd counted the nineteenth star, she was fast asleep.

Carole drifted off too, leaving Stevie the only Saddle Clubber awake. Stevie leaned up on her elbow and watched the grown-ups get settled on the other side of the dimming campfire. She smiled and shook her head. It had been up and down, she thought, but her parents were starting to get the hang of things. Tomorrow was the drive—that might be a different story.

Stevie lay back down and snuggled into her sleeping bag. Just as she drifted off, she thought she heard a call of some sort in the distance. Was it a coyote? Or just the wind? She couldn't keep herself awake long enough to wait for it to come again. She didn't hear the high, mournful sound when it pierced the silence again a moment later, nor did she hear the screeching answer of an eagle in the black distance.

Lisa opened one eye. The sky was a dark, rich blue, like cobalt-colored glass. An owl hooted softly in the distance. She closed her eyes, then opened them again. Now she remembered she was sleeping outside, in the middle of Colorado, under a big sky. The cattle drive was today.

She sat up and looked around. She could see Walter and a few of the parents already getting up and out of their sleeping bags and heading down to the creek. She quickly changed clothes in the warmth of her sleeping bag and got up. "Wake up, you cowgirls!" she said, nudging her sleeping friends before heading down to the creek to wash up.

By the time the sun edged its way up from behind the acres of cows, the whole group was up.

Mr. Atwood eyed his breakfast—beef jerky—skeptically. Finally, he bit off a hunk and chewed. After he swallowed it, he cleared his throat and said to his wife, "Mmm. Honey, you should serve this stuff at home!"

Mrs. Atwood worked quietly on her own portion. "Kind of spicy," she said between chews.

Mr. Lake laughed. "I thought you ate this junk only if you didn't have a fire nearby. Sort of like K rations."

Walter looked up from the coffee he was pouring out. "No point in bacon and eggs today—too much to do before the drive. Takes too big a fire."

"Bigger than what you need for coffee?" Mr. Atwood said.

"Oh, come on, Richard," said his wife. "You won't starve."

"Well, this is supposed to hold us—"

"Sure is tasty," Colonel Hanson said. "First you eat 'em, then you drive a herd of 'em. Mmm."

When Carole heard that, she practically choked on

hers. "I'll never look at a cow the same way again," she said to Kate.

"Well, wranglers," said Walter, "it's an authentic wrangler's breakfast."

"I'll take a little more coffee to wash down all that local flavor," said Mr. Lake, holding his mug out to Walter.

Lisa glanced away from the grown-ups. Their teasing was getting more than a little annoying. She heard Carole talking to her father about the topic on the way over to wash out coffee mugs, and she was glad Carole had picked up on their snooty tone too.

"What's the deal, Dad?" said Carole. "Does it have to be bacon and eggs for you too, every morning?"

"No, honey. But don't you think beef jerky is *too* authentic?"

Carole squinted at her father. "What do you mean by that?"

"Don't you think they're humoring us dudes a little bit?"

"Well, beef jerky is quick, light to carry along, and convenient. And besides, what's wrong with authenticity anyway? I mean, Dad, we couldn't very well bring a cappuccino machine and muffin tins."

"Mmm-hmm."

"Just think of the pots and pans you'd have to wash," Carole added.

"I love washing pots and pans!" said her father.

"Dad. The whole point is to ride well, pack light, make it easy on the horses—"

"Ah, yes, the horses," he said.

"Stop teasing, it's true."

"Okay. But for a short cattle drive like this, does it really make a difference how *easy* we go on the horses?"

"Sure it does," said Carole. "After all, you never know how hard they're going to have to work once the drive gets under way. Or how hard *you're* going to have to work, for that matter."

"But, Carole, honey, come on. Don't you think Walter and John could do this drive by themselves? Easily? To me it feels a little staged, that's all."

"I know, we felt that way on our first drive before it began. But we didn't feel that way for long. After all, it's real cattle we're moving, over real range. And most important, it's on—"

"I know," her father said, and they both said "real horses" at the same time.

Carole knew she was taking things a bit too seriously,

but she was glad she'd said something to her father. The parents' making fun of the food and drive had hurt her feelings a bit. And she was worried they'd hurt Walter and John too. Maybe once the cattle drive started, the Saddlebags would start taking things more seriously.

"WHAT'S WRONG, MOM?" Lisa asked. Her mother frowned as she drank her morning coffee.

"Oh, nothing, really."

Lisa wasn't convinced. "You haven't smiled once since you got up."

"Well, I didn't sleep very well at all," Mrs. Atwood admitted. "Must've been the hard ground."

Lisa wasn't so sure about her mother's excuse. She thought the scowl might have more to do with Lisa's friendship with John Brightstar than the hard ground. Then again, she thought, her mother was not the outdoorsy type. Maybe she was telling the truth.

John came walking up. "Morning, Lisa. Morning, Mrs. Atwood. How'd everyone sleep last night?"

"Not so well, thanks," said Lisa's mother. "I don't feel rested at all. And this coffee hasn't helped a bit."

She took one more sip, then handed her empty coffee cup to John.

Lisa blinked. It was as if her mother thought he was a servant.

But John seemed to take it in stride. He took the cup and dumped it into the bucket of dirty dishes.

After finishing with her bedroll, Lisa gathered up the bucket of dirty dishes and headed down to the stream.

Her mother went with her. "I thought this was John's job, honey."

"We all pitch in," she stated, struggling to hide her annoyance. "And since John's with the horses right now, it's our job." She handed her mother a towel.

Her mother didn't say another word.

Later, when they were all waiting to mount up, Lisa's mother took her bedroll over to Spot.

"Lisa, dear," she called. "Don't you think John should've saddled our horses first, before getting his own horse ready?"

John had saddled Tex and tied his lead to a tree, then gone on to saddle up the other horses. Walter and Carole were helping, and it wasn't taking too long.

"Oh, Mom, can't you be a little more patient?" Lisa grumbled.

"It's just that this bedroll is getting heavy," said Mrs. Atwood.

"Well, put it on the ground, then!" This time Lisa didn't even try to control her temper.

FINALLY THEY BROKE camp, put out the fire, and secured all bedrolls and equipment behind the saddles.

"May I have everyone's attention for a minute?" Walter asked.

Everyone gathered around, like teammates listening to their coach before a game.

"Now, you must remember that every cattle drive *can* be challenging. You just never know. Don't get lazy, or stop being alert, because that's always the time things tend to go wrong."

Colonel Hanson and Mr. Lake nodded politely.

"The less experienced riders," Walter went on, "should make sure you stick with riders who've spent more time on horseback. Okay, everybody, let's mount up."

"I don't see what could possibly go wrong," Mr. Lake mumbled as he climbed aboard his horse.

Colonel Hanson shrugged. "Strategic maneuvers," he said. "After you've herded humans all over the world, cows should be a piece of cake."

Mr. Lake and the colonel started heading their horses

84

over to the herd. Walter trotted past them to take the lead, and the others followed behind.

They were off.

As the group approached, the herd started slowly walking away from the horses. Walter picked up the pace a bit, and the cattle followed suit, breaking into a loud chorus of moos as they walked faster and trotted along. Then Walter rode to the front of the herd, leaving the others to watch for strays along the sides.

Lisa and John rode together along one side of the lowing herd, and they both spotted a tiny baby calf that had stopped to sniff a bush. When the dogie looked up, his mother was long gone. He raised his little head and started bleating anxiously.

"Time to rescue this little fella," said John as Tex broke into a lope. He rode up behind the calf to urge it along, and Lisa rode up alongside it to keep it from moving away from the herd. Together, with words of encouragement, they steered the dogie back to the herd, where his mother was now looking around anxiously for him. The cow and calf stopped so baby could nurse briefly. Lisa and John stayed close to them in case they got separated again.

Carole found herself trotting beside Mr. Atwood.

"Hey, look over there," she cried, pointing off to the southwest. "A stray." Carole started heading off in the stray steer's direction.

"Need some help?" called Mr. Atwood.

"Sure." Carole was in a lope by this time. Mr. Atwood rode beside her, and soon they had caught up to the steer, who seemed lost in thought, munching on a patch of greenish-brown scrub grass. Carole circled around the animal, and Mr. Atwood stayed behind him.

He stopped grazing and looked up.

"Hey, you," called Carole to the steer, "don't you know where the party is?" With the horses moving behind him, the steer got the message and started trotting off to join the rest.

"So that's how a roundup is done," cried Mr. Atwood.

"If you're lucky," Carole answered with a smile.

They rode on, keeping their eyes open.

On the other side of the herd, Mr. Lake told Walter, "I just spotted an animal that might need your help."

Sure enough, off to the left and just ahead of the herd was a steer who had gotten his horns caught in a bramble bush. The beast was trapped, head down, mooing loudly.

They trotted over to the animal's side. Walter dismounted and gave his reins to Mr. Lake. "Hold these, and try to keep my horse between you and that steer, just in case he gets any wild and crazy notions in his head."

But as soon as Walter walked up, patted the animal on its shoulders, and spoke to it quietly, the steer seemed to calm down. Then Walter took out his jackknife and quickly cut the bramble bush away.

The steer looked around and trotted off to join the herd.

"That was simple," said Walter as he remounted his horse.

"You make it look simple," said Mr. Lake with a smile of admiration, and they followed the steer back toward the herd.

Mrs. Lake and Colonel Hanson had slowed to a walk and let their horses lag toward the back of the herd.

Farther in back of them, bringing up the rear, rode Stevie and Stewball. She could hear snippets of their conversation—"loves secrets."

Hmm, she thought. What could they possibly be talking about? Then she heard her own name. They were talking about her! She rode a little closer, straining to hear better.

Colonel Hanson laughed. "Of course I know how well she keeps secrets. Remember when I decided to buy Carole a horse? Not only did Stevie and Lisa help me find Starlight, they kept the whole thing a secret all before Christmas, while I had Judy the vet make sure Starlight was the right choice!"

Stevie beamed to herself. She did love secrets, and Colonel Hanson's big Christmas present to Carole had been one of her all-time favorites.

"But that was a good secret," Mrs. Lake said.

Uh-oh. Stevie rode a bit closer.

Mrs. Lake chuckled. "Once she hid Michael's pet iguana in her room for a month! Michael was a mess!"

So was my room, Stevie thought to herself. But it hadn't been a month, it was much more like a week. She restrained herself from going over and setting her mother straight. She couldn't—she wanted to hear more.

Mrs. Lake went on. "But then there *was* the time she got all our kids to pitch in and make me the most incredible scrapbook for my birthday. They must have worked on it for months without a peep. What a lovely surprise!"

Her mother was exaggerating again, Stevie thought. It

hadn't taken months. But for the record, Stevie would leave that one alone anyway.

"Did you ever hear the one about some craziness she got into out here at a rodeo?" the colonel asked.

"No," her mother said.

"Well, maybe you're not supposed to hear that one. . . ."

They were having so much fun swapping stories about her antics, they never noticed Stevie riding closer and closer.

This is lots more fun than listening to my dad sing, Stevie thought as she rode along.

The only distraction came from Stevie's stomach, which had started reminding her that it was lunchtime. Up ahead, at the top of a small hill, she saw Parson's Rock slicing the sky. Then she noticed Walter pull out from in front of the herd and start heading up to the rock. Stevie rode around the herd to find her friends. She was glad they'd be stopping soon for lunch. It had been the scene of one of her favorite moments on her first trip to the Bar None, her surprise birthday party. And what's more, she was mighty hungry.

*       *       *

THE GROUP RODE up to the base of the rock and tethered their horses. While they stretched and rested, Carole and Kate passed out peanut butter and jelly sandwiches and lemonade.

Stevie wolfed down her sandwich and stood up. "Hey," she said to her friends, "let's go up to the top of the rock."

"You take your time down here," Carole said to the parents, "we'll be back in a bit."

"Nooooo problem," said her father, munching on his sandwich and sitting with his back against the rock.

The four girls clambered up to the top of the rock, which was flat and had enough room for them to sit in a circle.

"Perfect time and place for a club meeting," said Kate.

"So what do you think?" answered Carole. "How's it going so far?"

"You mean for us, or for the Saddlebags?" Lisa asked.

"Both."

"Well, I'm having fun," Lisa said. "Mostly because I've managed to stay far, far away from my mom."

"Why? What's up with your mom?" Carole asked.

"She's getting on my nerves. She's treating John like he's some kind of servant, and it's really embarrassing."

"Talk about embarrassing," Stevie answered. "My mom and Carole's dad spent the entire morning telling stories about *me*."

"How do you know?" Carole asked.

"They were right in front of me." She grinned. "I didn't want to listen, but I couldn't help myself."

"Listen, you guys," said Kate. "I think the ride's going very well so far. Every single Saddlebag has done some good work on this drive."

"You're right," Carole acknowledged. "Lisa, your dad was really getting the hang of things today. He even helped me rescue a stray." She shook her head and her expression darkened. "But my dad? He spent the whole morning chit-chatting at the back of the herd. Come on! I almost wish something would come up that would teach him a lesson or two. About real riding, and what goes into it."

Lisa nodded. "I know what you mean."

"Everybody mount up!" Walter's call came from the bottom of the rock.

The four girls stood up and looked over the edge of the rock. Everyone was getting ready to go. They hurried down the craggy rock to their horses.

Carole kept her thoughts to herself as she swung her

leg over and sat comfortably in Berry's saddle. Whatever happens happens, she thought. Why should I need my father to understand so much about riding anyway? After all—it comes down to how *I* feel about riding, and that part's just fine. In just a couple of hours, this beautiful ride will be over, and we'll be back at the Bar None.

She gave Parson's Rock a farewell glance and trotted over to catch up with the cattle.

BY THE EARLY AFTERNOON, the group had reached the arroyo they had come over yesterday. Only now, on the way back with the hundreds of cattle, Carole thought the descent into the streambed seemed much steeper. She watched as Walter led the first few steers down the side of the gully to drink at the narrow stream. The animals directly behind his horse made it down the bank okay, but the others got distracted and started to spread out on the high ground, looking for places to go down the hill.

Carole immediately saw the problem. The safest place

for the cattle to go down the hill was very narrow. Walter and John were guiding the cattle, but they had to funnel them practically one at a time into the narrow spot to take a drink.

As the other animals wandered off and tried to make their own way down to the water, some of them slipped on the steep embankment. This could lead to trouble, Carole realized.

"This is a job for Stewball!" she called to Stevie. "You two need to go down there and convince those cows not to spend the whole day drinking. I'll stay here with Berry and guide these cattle down the bank one at a time."

"Gotcha!" Stevie called back to her friend, and she and Kate headed to the front of the line of cattle, which was much farther upstream by now.

Stewball was a champion cutting horse. He could easily get cattle to go where he wanted, no matter what the situation was. Stevie knew this about Stewball, and she had the technique to take advantage of his skills.

When they got to the front of the line of cattle, Stevie and Stewball nudged, cajoled, and led the thirsty animals over to where Walter and John were trying to herd them up the bank.

One by one, and sometimes two by two, Carole let the

cattle go down. Lisa backed her up, making sure none of the cows wandered away.

Once they reached the stream, the animals stopped to drink for a long time. The youngest of them couldn't decide whether to drink from the stream or from their mothers, so they stood at their mothers' sides, alternately nursing and drinking the cool clear stream water.

It was a slow process. All The Saddle Club members stayed intensely focused on the job at hand.

"These ornery beasts are sure taking their time," said Colonel Hanson. He had been riding back and forth on the near bank.

Carole overheard her father. They're not being ornery, she thought with irritation. They're just thirsty.

But all of the Saddlebags were getting restless. Carole heard them continue to complain.

"What's going on down there?" Mr. Lake asked his wife and Mrs. Atwood, who had been sitting on their horses and chatting.

"The cows are having their coffee break," Mrs. Lake replied, "and it's taking forever."

"Sure is," Colonel Hanson agreed as he rode back up to the group, followed by Mr. Atwood. "You know, Rich and I were thinking, maybe us Saddlebags could do a little exploring up the banks here, while the experts get these cows squared away."

"Sounds like a good idea," said Mrs. Lake. "Let's clear it with the boss."

"Okey-doke," said her husband, and he rode down the steep bank. "How's it going?" he called to Walter.

"Fine." Walter looked up. "Slow but sure."

"Okay if us oldsters go exploring along the arroyo?"

"Yup," Walter answered. "Just don't go too far. Fifteen minutes up and fifteen back ought to bring you back by the time we've got all these critters on the other side."

"Okay," answered Mr. Lake. "See you in a few."

Walter kept on with his work.

Mr. Lake rode up to the rest of the grown-ups. "Walter says we've got a half hour till they're done watering the beasts," he said. "So I say we follow Mitch's plan and explore the wild expanse!"

Carole didn't say anything. But inside she wasn't so sure about "Mitch's plan." What if the parents didn't get back in time and Walter and John had to wait for them? Would the herd wait? Maybe the wranglers would have to go on ahead, and Carole and the girls would get stuck waiting for the parents.

They're not being very considerate, she thought. But

she was too busy with her job herding the cattle to stop and argue with her father.

The Saddlebags trotted off upstream alongside the bank of the arroyo.

AT THE BOTTOM of the arroyo Stevie and Kate had succeeded in moving dozens of cattle up toward Walter. But there were still quite a few to go. As the cows continued to descend, a calf got separated from his mother and scampered back up the first bank to try to find her.

"Oh, no, you don't," called Stevie as she and Stewball quickly got in front of the little thing and turned him around. "Back to Mama. She's down here anyway."

Sure enough, the mother looked up from her drink and started mooing fiercely for her baby to come back. That made Stevie and Stewball's job much easier.

"There you go," said Stevie as she reunited mother and baby.

A few minutes later there were only a few more cows waiting to come down. "Looks like we're almost done," Stevie called to Carole and Lisa.

"Finally," answered Carole. "I could use a drink myself." She pulled a small canteen off the back of her saddle and took a swig.

They all watched as Walter and John guided the last of the cows up the far bank.

"Sure took a while, didn't it?" said Lisa.

"Yeah. It's getting dark already," said Kate.

Stevie looked at her watch. "It's only three-thirty."

"That's weird," said Carole.

All four looked up at the sky. Above them was a low ceiling of sinister-looking clouds.

"Wow," Carole gasped. "I didn't see *those* coming."

"Uh-oh. I feel a drop," Stevie said.

Quickly, everyone reached for their ponchos.

Just as the last girl pulled her poncho over her head, the drops started coming down faster. A moment later the heavens opened and the rain clattered down in sheets. Soon it was as if they were standing in a wall of water. The land, which had been dry and parched, was instantly flooded. The rain kept coming down, pelting the girls' ponchos and horses. The horses just stood there, blinking under the barrage of raindrops.

"Woohoo!" cried Carole. It was as if she were standing in a waterfall. Berry started prancing nervously around. Carole adjusted her poncho to make sure it covered her saddle as well, and fixed her hood so the water would drain the right way off her visor. "I need a drain-pipe," she called to Lisa.

Lisa was pulling her pant legs out of her boots. "Me too," she hollered.

"Whaaaaaat?" cried Stevie. With the rain pounding down, they could hardly hear each other.

"I can't even see Berry's feet anymore!" Carole shouted.

Lisa adjusted her poncho so that it covered as much of Chocolate as possible. It was pouring, and she knew if the rain didn't let up, it would make the rest of the drive treacherous and painstaking.

The girls rode over to the top of the steepest rise and looked down.

"Wow!" cried Stevie in awe. "This is incredible!"

The tiny winding creek where they had watered the cattle was rapidly swelling upward.

"It's coming down by the bucketful!" Kate shouted.

Stevie held cupped hands out over Stewball's neck. They were instantly filled. "Hey, look at this!" she called. "Too bad we don't have shampoo!" She made lathering motions in Stewball's soaked mane.

Suddenly Lisa's horse slipped a bit as the earth under-neath her gave way. Lisa and Chocolate scrambled up to the flat part of the bank. The other riders moved up too. The stream was rapidly becoming a river, eating away what was left of the steep bank.

"It's good we got the cattle out of there before the storm," called Carole.

"I hope the Saddlebags get to see this!" Stevie shouted.

"Where are our parents anyway?" Carole cried, looking around. Walter had told them to ride for about thirty minutes, and it had been nearly an hour since they rode off. Suddenly Carole's stomach turned over.

The current below had torn a small tree out of the bank by its roots and sent it floating downstream. Behind it, rushing toward them, was a big black cowboy hat with silver buckles and a leather strap.

"It's my father's hat!" Carole gasped. The hat snagged on the sapling, and white water bubbled and splashed around it.

"Oh, no," Stevie cried as she gazed at the colonel's bobbing hat. "Our parents must be in terrible trouble!"

IN A PANIC, Stevie looked all around. She had to get to Walter and John. Where were they? There was the herd—upland from the stream. To her relief, a second later, she spotted John heading back in the girls' direction.

"We need help!" she shouted as soon as he was within earshot. "Our parents are missing!"

"Look!" Lisa pointed to the river and Colonel Hanson's hat.

John's face paled. "They haven't come back yet?"

"No!" cried Carole.

"Let's go," John stated grimly. He turned and started riding upstream, along the bank.

Lisa gave Chocolate the signal to trot. He wouldn't. She squeezed hard with her legs. He kept walking. "Go! Go!" she cried. She signaled him again, but he refused to speed up.

"Come on!" Stevie was saying to Stewball, but he wasn't going any faster either.

"Footing's too bad," John called to them. "They can't go faster."

Even walking felt treacherous. With the rain pelting down on them, the riders pressed forward, looking upstream for any signs of the missing parents. Nothing met their eyes but the rushing water and rain.

Lisa kept her thoughts focused on Chocolate and managing the slippery terrain. She didn't dare think about what might have happened to her mother and father. Together The Saddle Club and John would find the parents—they just had to.

Suddenly John stopped Tex and turned to the girls. "Look up there!" he shouted, pointing upstream.

Just around a curve in the river stood a small island. It was a tiny patch of land jutting out of the rushing water. It held two scraggly trees.

Also perched on the island, huddled together on their horses, were five terrified adults. And the water surrounding them was rising by the minute.

"Mom! Dad!" Lisa shouted.

But the grown-ups didn't hear Lisa's call. Mrs. Atwood was struggling to control a frantic Spot. Her hair was plastered to her face by the pouring rain. Yellowbird was backing and bucking under Colonel Hanson, and Mr. Lake's horse, Melody, was nervously pawing the ground.

The other horses stood with their heads down, ears back, and the whites of their eyes showing. They were as frightened as their riders. Water streamed over their matted forelocks.

"Mom! Dad!" Lisa hollered again, waving. "Colonel Hanson!"

Mrs. Atwood finally spotted them and waved her arms frantically. "Help!" she shrieked. Spot was pulling on the reins, trying desperately to get off the tiny patch of land. Mrs. Atwood pulled back, but Spot kept stepping down the bank, slipping, then backing up again.

"Hold on to the pommel on the saddle, Mom!" Lisa shouted even louder. "Don't worry! We're coming to get you!"

John pulled his lariat out from under his poncho. It was still dry. Instantly he swung the rope over a boulder on a high ledge of the bank, farther upstream.

"Kate, make sure that end of the rope's secure," he called. "I'll try to get the other end around that tree." He pointed to one of the trees on the island.

"Lisa, come with me," he continued. "We don't know how deep this water is. The horses may have to swim. We need to start out upstream. Carole and Stevie, wait at the bottom of the bank here in case some of them get pulled by the current. You may have to ride out to catch them."

Stevie nodded grimly. Then she and Carole picked their way down the bank of the river.

John launched the other end of the rope high into the air. It arced up through the rain and came down on the branch of a tree near Mr. Lake.

Mr. Lake reached up, grabbed the rope, and secured it tightly to the tree.

"Help!" Mrs. Atwood screamed. Spot's eyes were wide, and his nostrils flared. His ears lay flat on his head.

Lisa watched in horror as the frightened horse plunged toward the raging water. "Hang on, Mom," she cried. "John's coming!" She didn't know if her mother heard her words. She only prayed her mother would know what to do.

In an instant John and Tex slid down the bank. Lisa watched in frozen terror. John leaned back in the saddle, and Tex slid straight down on his haunches. It was like the sliding stops she'd seen them do, only this time it wasn't for show. It was to save her mother's life. She tightened her grip on Chocolate's reins.

When John and Tex reached the river, the water was up to Tex's knees. Carefully John guided Tex into the currents, toward the downstream part of the island. Lisa could see him talking to the horse with every step, encouraging him, calming him, assuring him. Even so, they moved fast.

Lisa's mother was trying to stay in her saddle and keep Spot from heading into the white water.

Lisa called again to her mother. "Don't lean forward! Sit back, or you'll fall off!"

Mrs. Atwood leaned forward more, straining to hear Lisa in the din of the pouring rain. Spot lurched forward. Lisa waved her arms. Then, realizing her mother couldn't hear, she did the only thing possible. She leaned back in her saddle, trying to demonstrate her point.

Mrs. Atwood got it. She sat back in the saddle. Lisa sighed with relief. Her mother stayed on.

John and Tex moved into the deeper water, which swirled around Tex's shoulders. Then Tex began to swim. His head and neck stretched out and his body moved against the furious current. John guided him toward the island.

Lisa held her breath as Spot lunged forward and entered the swirling white water.

John grabbed Spot's reins. "Here, give me those." Then he looked Mrs. Atwood straight in the eye. "You're going to be all right. Please stay calm. I'm going to lead you through the water, and your horse is going to start to swim. It might feel funny at first, but it's the only way out of this alive. I'll be leading you, and whatever happens, I won't let go of the reins. But you have to stay on your horse. Do you understand? Hold the pommel of the saddle, and grip Spot with your legs."

Lisa's mother nodded silently. She looks exhausted, Lisa thought. I hope she can hang on.

Together John and Mrs. Atwood started moving toward the bank where Lisa was waiting. She could see that the water surrounding them was deep. Luckily, Spot seemed to calm down the minute Tex started leading him, and he swam easily toward her.

"Oh!" Mrs. Atwood exclaimed. She and Spot glided along behind Tex and John, the horse's head bobbing above the water.

As they approached, Lisa headed sideways down the slippery bank. Her mother seemed to be losing her balance. "Mom, lean forward now!" Lisa called. "John, she's falling!" Mrs. Atwood sat forward and grabbed the saddle pommel.

The two horses finally reached the bank. John reached up and grabbed the rope he'd strung across the water. "Here," he said, forcing it into Mrs. Atwood's hand. "Use this to pull yourself up."

Mrs. Atwood leaned forward and tried to pull herself along with the rope. But the saddle pommel gave her better leverage, so she went back to using it to stay on Spot's back.

Finally, with tears and rain streaming down her face, Mrs. Atwood reached the spot where Lisa was waiting.

"Here." John tossed Lisa the reins to her mother's horse. "Take her up to the top, and then come back and give me a hand with the others."

Lisa nodded. "It's okay, Mom. You're okay now," she

said, choking back her own sobs. John pivoted around and slid back down into the water.

The island was being swallowed by water. The four parents remaining on the small plot of land were trying not to panic, but Carole could tell from her father's face that he was very anxious. His expression grew even more frightened when Yellowbird whinnied and pawed at the mud, then started to buck.

When John reached the island again, he mounted the upstream banks and grabbed Yellowbird's reins.

"Grab the pommel and sit back," John yelled. "We've got no time to lose. Just follow me."

Carole rode upstream, turned, and slid down into the water. She couldn't just watch—she had to do something. She guided Berry against the current. When the horse's feet left the ground and he started struggling against the current, she felt strangely suspended. But she had no time to think about it. John and her father were swimming toward her. John handed her Yellowbird's reins, then turned Tex back around and headed toward the island.

"Come on, Dad," said Carole, "we're almost across."

Their horses soon found footing on land again, and climbed up out of the water.

Back on the island, Mr. Lake seemed to have Melody under fairly good control. He headed next down the bank to meet John, sliding with rocks and mud and rain into the water.

But as he went, Melody slipped and tumbled on her knees. Mr. Lake let go of the reins and went right over her head, splashing into the water. He flailed his arms as the current spun him around and swept him downstream.

"Dad!" cried Stevie. She'd been waiting downstream. Now she pivoted Stewball and urged him down into the water.

Stewball plunged into the white foam. Water swirled around the tops of his legs and splashed into Stevie's boots as the two of them moved into the deeper water. Mr. Lake was moving toward them.

Stevie whipped her poncho over her head and tossed one end to her father. He reached out to grab it, and Stevie held tight to her end with both hands.

Quickly she wrapped the poncho around the pommel of her saddle, then signaled Stewball with her legs. That was all he needed. The horse turned back to shore, carrying Stevie on his back and towing Mr. Lake behind them.

Without a poncho Stevie was drenched in a second. Rain streamed down her back. But she barely noticed. Every ounce of her concentration focused on clutching the poncho rope. Her father's life depended on it.

Finally they reached the bank. Stewball started to climb up out of the river. Stevie stopped him and dismounted to pull her father up on shore.

Father and daughter collapsed in the wet rocks and mud.

"Dad, are you all right?" Stevie gasped.

"Yes," he managed to say. "Thanks to you."

"And Stewball." Stevie fought back the tears. "Think you can climb on him?" she said. "We have to get you farther up this bank, and it'll be easier on Stewball than trying to hike it on foot."

"Okay." Mr. Lake got up and Stevie helped him into the saddle. "Now lean forward, and crisscross your way up. You should stay on—this time."

Mr. Lake and Stewball started up. Stevie turned and looked back upstream. Kate was leading Mrs. Lake through the water. Stevie sighed with relief to see her mother still on her horse. Her mother looked at her and gave her a grim thumbs-up. After them came Mr. Atwood, led by John. Carole had come back down to wait in the shallow water at the edge in case anyone needed help.

Stevie's mother leaned forward as her horse followed Moonglow and Kate up the steep bank. Mrs. Lake clutched the horse's soaked mane.

Just then Stevie noticed another commotion in the water. Mr. Atwood's horse, Tripper, had slipped going up the bank, and Mr. Atwood was starting to come out of his saddle.

Carole pivoted Berry so that he came up alongside Tripper. She wedged herself up against the horse so there was nowhere for Mr. Atwood to fall.

"Drop the reins. Grab your saddle," Carole commanded. "Pull yourself back on."

Mr. Atwood did what she said, but the saddle started to slip with his weight.

The girth must be loose from all this water, Carole realized. Quickly, she leaned out of her saddle and said, "Ready, one, two, three!" and gave Mr. Atwood a huge push. Berry moved sideways with the impact, but he kept his balance in the foamy water. Mr. Atwood was back in the saddle. Carole couldn't believe she'd found the strength to do it.

Carole glanced upstream, where Stevie was trying to

climb up the muddy bank. She clung to a root and was grabbing for another.

"Can you make it?" Carole yelled.

"I think so!" Stevie hollered back. As the rain continued to pelt her, she pulled her way up the muddy hill.

When she reached the top, Stevie saw her father leading Stewball over to her. He looked at Stevie, who was completely drenched.

"I think it's a little late for this," he said, holding out Stevie's wrinkled, twisted, wet poncho.

She laughed. It felt good to laugh.

She took the reins from her father and mounted her horse. Her jeans made a squishing sound as she sat in the saddle. Water oozed over the tops of her boots. Every inch of her was soaked. Her hair dripped down the back of her shirt, but she couldn't really tell, because her shirt was so wet. Stevie looked at her father. She didn't know how this was possible, but he looked as if he was even wetter than she was. Then she remembered, he'd gone for a swim—with all his clothes on.

The rain had slackened some, but it was still falling hard. Stevie pushed the hair out of her eyes and looked up the bank to see the others riding toward them.

"What a wet group!" she called out. Everyone was

dripping. Water ran off people's eyelashes, down their noses, down their boots, and off their stirrups. The horses' tails were waterlogged and hung like snakes on their flanks.

"Look!" cried Lisa. Everyone looked toward the island. Only now nothing was left. The flooding waters had completely engulfed the patch of land.

"Talk about the nick of time," Colonel Hanson said soberly.

The riders watched the raging river for another minute, each one realizing how close they'd come to disaster. Finally John turned Tex in the direction of the herd, and the wet, weary riders headed off to find Walter.

When Carole glanced back one last time at the flooded arroyo, her eyes streamed with tears. The memory of her father's silly cowboy hat floating downstream was almost too much to bear. She looked over at him now, and a sob caught in her throat. With her mother gone, he was everything—all the family—she had. What if she had lost him?

Ahead of Carole, Lisa was thinking similar thoughts. Just this afternoon she'd been furious at her mother. Now, after seeing her mother sliding into the white water, totally helpless and panicked, Lisa felt grateful and lucky to be riding beside her.

She may be a pain sometimes, Lisa thought, but she's still my mother.

Suddenly Mrs. Atwood reached over and grabbed Lisa's hand. The rain had stopped and off in the distance a rainbow glittered over the majestic Rockies.

"Look, honey," Mrs. Atwood said softly. "A rainbow. Isn't it beautiful?" Lisa just nodded, still too filled with feelings to speak.

For a moment all the riders watched the rainbow together. Then they continued on to where Walter and the herd were waiting. As they rode, the sun burst out from behind the clouds and slowly began to warm their dripping clothes and bodies.

BACK AT THE Bar None, the girls first took care of their exhausted horses, then headed to their bunkhouse to take care of themselves.

They all showered and changed into dry clothes.

Carole was combing out her thick black hair, when a knock came on the bunkhouse door.

"Anybody home?" It was a girl's voice.

"Christine!" Stevie cried.

Christine Lonetree, Kate's neighbor and the other member of The Saddle Club's Colorado branch, stepped inside. "I didn't think you'd still be in here this close to suppertime!"

"Well," answered Carole, pulling her hair into a barrette, "we had a long afternoon. But that's another story."

"What happened?" Christine asked.

Carole gave a shudder.

Lisa sniffed the air. "We'll tell you at dinner and later, when you sleep over," she said. "Right now I can't wait another minute for some of the Devines' barbecue!"

And as they stepped off the porch of their bunkhouse, the big triangle at the main house rang loud and long.

"WELCOME BACK TO all our drenched, exhausted cowpokes. Drive was more than you bargained for, I heard." Frank Devine placed the final platter, piled high with chicken, steak, and ribs, in the middle of the big table. "We loved having all of you with us this week. Here's to a safe trip home tomorrow—under sunny skies—and a speedy return to the Bar None sometime real soon!"

He took off his chef's apron. "Dig in!" he said, and they all did.

"So what happened this afternoon?" Christine asked.

Carole put down her corn on the cob and wiped her

hands on her napkin. She took a deep breath. "We all got caught in a flash flood."

"You did?" Christine said. "You were out in *that* rainstorm?"

Carole nodded. "And we weren't exactly expecting it."

"What do you mean?" asked Christine. "Didn't you pack your ponchos?"

"Yup," said Stevie, "and it's a good thing we did."

"Stevie used hers as a lifeline," explained Kate.

"A what?" Christine asked. She looked from Stevie to Carole to Kate to Lisa. "Okay. So what exactly happened?"

"Some of us got a little stuck in a creek bed," said Carole, "that kind of filled up with water. So some others of us helped out—"

"Don't underestimate yourselves!" boomed a voice from down the table. It was Colonel Hanson. Everyone else stopped talking.

"That's right, don't underestimate yourselves *or* the flood." Colonel Hanson put both his hands on the table, paused, and looked around at everyone. "There *was* a flash flood. And *some of us* didn't exactly get stuck, we goofed. It wasn't you girls. It was us dudes. We tried to ride where we had no business riding. They don't call us Saddlebags for nothing!"

There was a small titter from the girls' end of the table.

Colonel Hanson continued. "You see, we made an error of judgment that on any ordinary day might not have been so foolish. But in a flash flood, it was incredibly dangerous. We decided to see if we could all fit on top of this tiny hill in the middle of the arroyo. Then it started raining. The hill became an island. We panicked.

"And that's when The Saddle Club, and John, found us. *They* stayed calm, used good judgment and tremendous riding skills, and got us all out of danger, and up to the dry ground. If they hadn't found us . . ."

Colonel Hanson paused and swallowed hard. His eyes met Carole's, and he quickly looked down.

Carole looked around. All the other parents' eyes were glistening. Mr. Lake cleared his throat, and Mrs. Atwood put down her fork.

Colonel Hanson took a deep breath. "Matter of fact," he said quietly, "I'm not sure any of us Saddlebags would *be* here tonight if it weren't for our daughters and John Brightstar." He looked up, smiled, and raised his glass.

"So I propose a toast to our wonderful daughters—the smartest young women on horseback!"

"Hear, hear!" said Mr. Lake. Everyone raised a glass.

"And to John Brightstar," Colonel Hanson continued, "a terrific wrangler and horseman, and a fine young man! John, may you win *only* blue ribbons in your horse shows. You did more special riding today than anyone'll ever see at a rodeo."

All raised their glasses once again. John blushed a little.

Mrs. Atwood suddenly spoke up. "I also want to thank you, John, for thinking fast and keeping me and my horse from swimming all the way to Texas!"

Everyone laughed.

"I think I understand now," Lisa's mother continued, "that when my daughter says riding is serious fun, she means riding is *both* serious *and* fun."

Stevie raised her mug of soda. "I'll drink to that!" she said.

"Amen," said Carole under her breath.

Lisa caught her mother's eye and winked.

TAP, TAP, TAP.

In her sleep Stevie stirred.

*Tap, tap, tap.*

This time the noise awakened her.

Christine was already up, looking around. "I think someone's at the door," she said quietly.

Stevie sat up and pulled on her robe. She slowly opened the door and peered around it.

"Good morning!" said a low voice.

"Colonel Hanson!" Stevie exclaimed.

Carole sat up in bed.

"Is something wrong?" asked Stevie.

"No, not at all," replied the colonel with a smile. "Us 'Bags just wanted to know if you'd like to take us on a bareback sunrise ride. It's our last chance before going home."

"You bet!" cried Carole.

"Just give us two minutes to get dressed," said Stevie.

"Meet you at the barn," replied Carole's father, and he left.

Lisa got up and scampered to the window. "It's still dark. I can't believe they all got up this early!"

The girls quickly pulled on their jeans and shirts and boots and headed out to the barn.

All the parents were standing at the barn door, waiting.

"Let me cut our horses," said Kate as she went inside to get a bridle for Moonglow.

"I think you might want to use saddles," Carole said to the parents. "Sometimes it's hard to keep your balance when you're riding bareback, so you'll have more fun on this ride if you use saddles."

Mrs. Atwood smiled. "This time I think I'll take The Saddle Club's advice. I'd much rather enjoy the ride than be worrying about whether or not I'm going to stay on."

"I agree," added her husband. "Bareback riding takes more skills than I've got, even after yesterday's intensive lesson."

Soon all horses were ready, the grown-ups' horses with saddles and bridles, the girls' horses with bridles only. The Saddlebags mounted up, and waited until the girls could join them.

Mounting with a stirrup was easy, but stirrups came attached to saddles, and bareback riding came with none. Mounting a horse bareback usually required a boost.

The girls were all experienced bareback riders by now, but Stevie remembered her first time riding bareback, and how hard it had been to keep her balance on the horse without a saddle. She was glad the grown-ups were using saddles. It took only a few minutes until the girls were ready.

The group rode off toward the hills, under a sapphire predawn sky.

Christine and Stevie led the way out of the valley and up into the hills. It was the same ride Christine had taken them on when they first met her, on their very first stay at the Bar None.

They rode slowly, taking care on the rocky, twisting path. As they ascended, the sky turned paler and paler blue.

Finally Christine and Stevie reached the summit. They rode along the hill's crest a bit to make room for the others. Stevie watched as her parents rounded the last turn and reached the top.

Over the edge of the eastern horizon was a wash of pink and purple clouds.

"Perfect timing!" Stevie exclaimed.

A thin orange crescent peeked over the horizon, and as they watched, it became bigger and bigger, until it was a half circle.

"If you look this way, you can see the ranch," said Lisa.

Her mother rode up beside her and looked out over the valley. "Oh, yes," she said, "there it is!"

Under the bright sky, now striped with pink and orange, they saw the ranch, the barn, and the outbuildings.

"They're so tiny from here—" said Mrs. Atwood, "look at that dog."

Lisa and her mother watched as a speck of a dog ran out from the Bar None barn toward the corral. Then a miniature rider came out into the corral, mounted on a tiny horse.

"That must be John," said Mrs. Atwood. They watched the rider start to work the horse around the corral.

"I think it is," said Lisa.

"He's quite a good rider," said Mrs. Atwood, "isn't he?"

"He sure is," said Lisa, smiling as she watched the distant horseman. She looked at her mother and gave a little laugh. "He sure is."

STEVIE SAT ON Stewball, between her mother and father. They didn't say much, just watched as the sky lightened and the deep rich orange and purple and pink faded into the daylight. This time Stevie's father didn't even sing. He scanned the whole view, then turned to Stevie and said, "Thanks for throwing me a line yesterday."

Stevie didn't know what to say. She bit her lip and looked from her mother to her father. "Thank you, Dad, and Mom," she said softly. "For bringing me out here, and for coming along."

"Any time," said her father.

"SO THIS IS what you and Frank Devine have been raving about, hmm?" Colonel Hanson teased his daughter.

"Yes," answered Carole. "Don't you think it was worth getting up early for?"

"Sure it was," he answered. "Better than the movie *Shane*."

Carole raised her eyebrows. "I never thought I'd hear you say you like something better than a Western," she teased him gently.

He smiled at her. "Being here, and sharing this with my daughter is worth much more than all the Westerns in the world," he answered.

Unexpectedly tears sprung into Carole's eyes. She reached over and squeezed his hand. Then the two of them were quiet, letting the beauty and expanse of the panorama say all that needed to be said.

A FEW MINUTES later Mr. Lake finally broke the riders' silence. "Anyone else hungry enough to eat a . . . horse?"

"I don't know about your choice of entrée," said Stevie, "but I'm starved too! Let's head down."

Carole and Kate led the group back.

When they reached the valley, Stevie stopped and pointed. "Why don't you Saddlebags ride ahead and wait for us by that big tree over there, just before the corral. That way, we can have a bareback race and you can be the judges!"

"Okay," agreed Mr. Lake. The girls watched as the Saddlebags trotted through the last stretch of valley.

When the parents had reached the tree, the girls lined up.

"On your marks!" said Stevie. "Get set, go!"

They were off. The girls kicked their horses into a lope, then, one by one, they leaned forward and grabbed their horses' manes. The horses knew what was up, and sprinted into a gallop. Carole was in the lead, and Stevie and Stewball were in the rear. Stewball put his head down and picked up speed. He seemed to know where they were headed, and as usual, he had some tricks in store. While all the others galloped ahead, Stewball turned right up a little rise.

Stevie leaned forward and squeezed with her legs to stay on. Sure enough, he cut a few yards off the distance, and as they headed for the tree, Stewball and Stevie were now in front.

"Come on, Stevie!" Stevie heard her parents cheer.

Mr. and Mrs. Atwood were screaming, "Go, Lisa, go! You can do it!"

Carole's father sat on his horse and clapped and shouted, "Look at her go! Come on, baby, come ooooon!"

"Yeeee—hah!" cried Mr. Lake as Stevie pulled up first. She gave Stewball a big hug and joined in the cheering as her friends rode in.

They walked their horses from there to the corral so they could cool down.

John was waiting there for them, leaning on the corral fence.

"I think Mrs. Devine's cooking up the breakfast to top all breakfasts," he said, "so as soon as you can, you better head on in."

He helped the grown-ups with their saddles, and they all watered and fed their horses. Then the whole group headed for the main house, where the smell of bacon, eggs, coffee, and sticky buns hit them as they opened the door.

"I'm glad it's a huge breakfast," said Lisa. "That way we can put off packing a little longer."

Everyone agreed. In a few hours they'd be driving to the little airport where Frank Devine would fly The Saddle Club and the Saddlebags back to Willow Creek.

"Shhh," whispered Lisa. "Let me check if the coast is clear." She tiptoed out into the hallway. Inside her room, Carole and Stevie stifled giggles.

"So?" asked Stevie.

Lisa looked over her shoulder. "All clear. But, guys, let's try to keep *really* quiet. That way we can stay up as late as we want."

Dressed in their nightgowns, the three girls tiptoed one by one out of Lisa's room and down the stairs.

When they reached the kitchen, Stevie and Carole carefully pulled out chairs and sat at the kitchen table.

They started giggling conspiratorially again.

"Will you stop!" Lisa whispered as she filled a pot with milk and put it on the stove. She reached for the hot chocolate mix. "If you can't keep it down, we'll get caught, and there goes the hot chocolate!"

Stevie became very serious. Not getting caught was a point of honor with her.

When the cocoa was ready, each girl took a mugful, popped three marshmallows into it, and crept back upstairs. They were barely back in Lisa's room before they burst out laughing again.

"Shhhhhhh!"

*Knock knock knock.*

All mugs were quickly stashed in Lisa's closet.

"Yes?" Lisa said, trying to sound innocent.

"Can you young ladies please keep it down in there so we can pretend we don't know you're still awake?" said a deep voice.

"We'll do our best, Daddy. Sorry."

Mr. Atwood's footsteps padded back down the hall.

Stevie pulled the mugs back out of the closet. "Let's drink this stuff before it gets cold!" she whispered. She took a sip. "Mmm. Lisa, you make the best hot chocolate."

"This side of the Mississippi River," added Carole.

"Sounds like you miss the Bar None," Lisa said to Carole.

"Me too." Stevie blew softly into her cup.

"So how would you rate that vacation," Lisa asked her friends, "best one you ever took? Bar None?"

Stevie laughed. "No vacation at the Bar None can ever be a bomb. It definitely had its rough spots though."

"Yeah," said Carole, "like seeing Dad's hat floating downstream—"

"Without your dad underneath it," Stevie cut in.

"And my mom. Yank and kick and kick some more. I mean, how embarrassing is that?" added Lisa. "But . . ."

"But . . . ," Carole echoed, "when you add it all up, they were good sports."

"You think so?" said Lisa.

"Yup, I really do. Even your mom got the hang of it after a while—she left that place a much better rider than when she came."

"Nothing like crossing a river in a flash flood to make you a better rider," Lisa answered.

"I was so glad to have Mom and Dad there," said Stevie, "after all the stories I'd told them!"

"The main thing is," added Carole, "they learned a whole lot more about horses and riding, and how much we love them, than they ever would here in Willow Creek."

They all nodded, quietly sipping their cocoa.

"The last thing Kate said to me," Carole went on, "was that we can all come back in the summer if we like."

"Oh," said Stevie, "that would be so great. But just *us*, right?"

"I think she meant our parents too."

Stevie groaned softly. "Once is enough."

"It may not have that same unpredictable magic the second time around," Carole agreed.

"Mom said she had fun," Lisa said. "You should have heard her today. She kept talking about what a nice boy that John What's-his-name is."

"All right!" said Carole.

"He took us all swimming on horseback," said Stevie, "and finally made the right impression."

"However, she did remark that she'd gotten a brochure for a nice Club Med vacation."

Stevie giggled. "*I* know. Let's send the parents to Club Med, and we can go back to the Bar None!"

"Yes!" Carole shouted.

"Shhh!" said Lisa.

"Whoa, one minor problem," said Stevie. "I don't think we should leave all your parents alone with my parents for a week."

"Why?"

"Because they'd sit around and entertain themselves talking about all the awful things I've done!"

"Stevie," Lisa pretended to chide her friend. "If you didn't do awful things, you wouldn't be Stevie!"

"And we wouldn't be The Saddle Club," Stevie concluded logically.

At that the girls clinked their nearly empty mugs together.

# ABOUT THE AUTHOR

BONNIE BRYANT is the author of more than sixty books for young readers, including novelizations of movie hits such as *Teenage Mutant Ninja Turtles* and *Honey, I Blew Up the Kid*, written under her married name, B. B. Hiller.

Bonnie Bryant began writing The Saddle Club in 1986. Although she had done some riding before that, she intensified her studies then, and found herself learning right along with her characters Stevie, Carole, and Lisa. She claims that they are all much better riders than she is.

Bonnie Bryant was born and raised in New York City. She lives in Greenwich Village with her two sons.

# Saddle Up For Fun!
# Join The Saddle Club

**As an official Saddle Club member you'll get:**

- *Saddle Club newsletter*
- *Saddle Club membership card*
- *Saddle Club bookmark*
- *and exciting updates on everything that's happening with your favorite series.*

Bantam Doubleday Dell Books for Young Readers
Saddle Club Membership Box BK
1540 Broadway
New York, NY 10036

SKYLARK

**Bantam Doubleday Dell**
Books for Young Readers

Name _____

Address _____

City _____ State _____ Zip _____

Date of birth _____

Offer good while supplies last.                    BFYR - 8/93

# THE SADDLE CLUB™

| | | |
|---|---|---|
| ❑ 15594-6 HORSE CRAZY #1 | $3.50/$4.50 Can. | |
| ❑ 15611-X HORSE SHY #2 | $3.25/$3.99 Can. | |
| ❑ 15626-8 HORSE SENSE #3 | $3.50/$4.50 Can. | |
| ❑ 15637-3 HORSE POWER #4 | $3.50/$4.50 Can. | |
| ❑ 15703-5 TRAIL MATES #5 | $3.50/$4.50 Can. | |
| ❑ 15728-0 DUDE RANCH #6 | $3.50/$4.50 Can. | |
| ❑ 15754-X HORSE PLAY #7 | $3.25/$3.99 Can. | |
| ❑ 15769-8 HORSE SHOW #8 | $3.25/$3.99 Can. | |
| ❑ 15780-9 HOOF BEAT #9 | $3.50/$4.50 Can. | |
| ❑ 15790-6 RIDING CAMP #10 | $3.50/$4.50 Can. | |
| ❑ 15805-8 HORSE WISE #11 | $3.25/$3.99 Can.. | |
| ❑ 15821-X RODEO RIDER #12 | $3.50/$4.50 Can. | |
| ❑ 15832-5 STARLIGHT CHRISTMAS #13 | $3.50/$4.50 Can. | |
| ❑ 15847-3 SEA HORSE #14 | $3.50/$4.50 Can. | |
| ❑ 15862-7 TEAM PLAY #15 | $3.50/$4.50 Can. | |
| ❑ 15882-1 HORSE GAMES #16 | $3.25/$3.99 Can. | |
| ❑ 15937-2 HORSENAPPED #17 | $3.50/$4.50 Can. | |
| ❑ 15928-3 PACK TRIP #18 | $3.50/$4.50 Can. | |

| | |
|---|---|
| ❑ 15938-0 STAR RIDER #19 | $3.50/$4.50 Can. |
| ❑ 15907-0 SNOW RIDE #20 | $3.50/$4.50 Can. |
| ❑ 15983-6 RACEHORSE #21 | $3.50/$4.50 Can. |
| ❑ 15990-9 FOX HUNT #22 | $3.50/$4.50 Can. |
| ❑ 48025-1 HORSE TROUBLE #23 | $3.50/$4.50 Can. |
| ❑ 48067-7 GHOST RIDER #24 | $3.50/$4.50 Can. |
| ❑ 48072-3 SHOW HORSE #25 | $3.50/$4.50 Can. |
| ❑ 48073-1 BEACH RIDE #26 | $3.50/$4.50 Can. |
| ❑ 48074-X BRIDLE PATH #27 | $3.50/$4.50 Can. |
| ❑ 48075-8 STABLE MANNERS #28 | $3.50/$4.50 Can. |
| ❑ 48076-6 RANCH HANDS #29 | $3.50/$4.50 Can. |
| ❑ 48077-4 AUTUMN TRAIL #30 | $3.50/$4.50 Can. |
| ❑ 48145-2 HAYRIDE #31 | $3.50/$4.50 Can. |
| ❑ 48146-0 CHOCOLATE HORSE #32 | $3.50/$4.50 Can. |
| ❑ 48147-9 HIGH HORSE #33 | $3.50/$4.50 Can. |
| ❑ 48148-7 HAY FEVER #34 | $3.50/$4.50 Can. |
| ❑ 48149-5 A SUMMER WITHOUT HORSES Super #1 | $3.99/$4.99 Can. |

**Bantam Doubleday Dell**
**Books For Young Readers**

Bantam Books, Dept. SC35,
2451 South Wolf Road, Des Plaines, IL 60018          DA60

Please send the items I have checked above. I am enclosing $_____ (please add $2.50 to cover postage and handling). Send check or money order, no cash or C.O.D.s please.

Mr/Ms _____

Address _____

City/State _____     Zip _____

Please allow four to six weeks for delivery.
Prices and availability subject to change without notice.          **SC35-4/94**